MW01634710

THE
F.L.I.G.H.T.
NETWORK

THE
F.L.I.G.H.T.
NETWORK

J. S. TOMAS

The F.L.I.G.H.T. Network
Copyright © 2020 by Johnathan S. Tomas

An imprint of Johnathan S. Tomas

All rights reserved.

No part of this book may be used or reproduced in any manner whatsoever without written permission.

This book is a work of fiction. Any references to historical events, real people, or real places are used fictitiously. Other names, characters, places, institutions, and events are products of the author's imagination, and any resemblance to actual events or places or persons, living or dead, is entirely coincidental, except for the character's John and Noelle Teslow, who are partly based off the author and his wife, Naveen.

Text copyright © Johnathan S. Tomas
Cover design copyright © Johnathan S. Tomas
Edited by Paul Fairbairn

Library and Archives Canada Cataloguing in Publication

ISBN: 978-1-7778906-0-5 (paperback), 978-1-7778906-1-2 (hardcover)

First Edition, 2021

*For my wife, Naveen, my son, Emmett, and the rest of the
Tomas family bubble, including Hershey boy*

Chapter One

Good morning, Noah Teslow. Today is your 18th birthday! Go out there and make it a great day. And don't forget to take your antidepressant pill.

The automated home audio system had the voice of an eloquent British male—dubbed Charles—but his cut-glass accent was muffled by the alarm wailing overhead.

Noah awoke, hyperventilating, his heart racing.

He'd experienced terrible and vivid dreams every night for the past week. Though the scenarios differed, they always ended the same way—with a bullet to Noah's head. Last night, a figure in a black HAZMAT suit and helmet had appeared, its tinted face-shield cracked down the center. The figure had removed its helmet and its blood-shot eyes had stared down at him. It pressed the muzzle of a gun directly to Noah's forehead. And fired.

The dreams shook him to the core but he kept silent about them. He didn't want to worry his busy father with such foolishness.

It was just a dream, he told himself and sank back into his pillow, relief washing over him.

His bedroom was still dark; through the half-shut blinds, parallel lines of moonlight fell onto the bed covers. Noah grabbed his pillow and pressed it to his ears, to block out the deafening alarm. The racket continued until he forced himself out of bed and stumbled over to the light switch to turn off the alarm button next to it. He just couldn't get used to an 8 a.m. wake-up call.

The moment the alarm fell silent, the bedroom was bathed in fluorescent light. Noah squinted and covered his eyes with his hand until his pupils adjusted to the brightness. The wall opposite his bed glimmered into life and the time and date scrolled across it: *8:01 a.m., Friday, November 22, C49+.*

He was stretching and in mid-yawn when the gears in his brain finally meshed. It was his birthday.

As he dressed, he looked out the circular window and watched the snow slowly drifting down from the sky. A typical wintery day in Saskatoon, Saskatchewan. The prairies were never kind during the winter months and the land was covered in a heavy blanket of snow for half a year. He decided not to think about the cold days ahead and focus on his eighteenth birthday, instead.

Once he was dressed, he opened the bottle of antidepressants on his nightstand and swallowed a Lumoxetine tablet in one gulp. Rolling his neck from side to side, he rode the escalator down from outside his room to the main floor and walked into the kitchen. The glistening white surfaces hurt his eyes almost as much as the fluorescent lights in his room.

"Good morning, sweetheart."

Noah's stepmom Jasmine was always the first one up in the mornings. She closed the stainless-steel refrigerator door and crossed the kitchen with a cup of steaming coffee in one hand. She had jet-black hair, bright hazel eyes, and natural olive skin. Her complexion was near-flawless—apart from the track marks on her arms.

Noah didn't know the full story, but what he did know was that she'd had a pretty tough upbringing, and she'd been involved with drugs. Somehow, she'd managed to turn that into something positive, by getting into college and studying pharmacology. She'd left her old life behind and became a pharmacist, which was how she'd met Noah's dad.

She regarded him closely. "How are you feeling this morning, birthday boy?"

She leaned over and smacked her lips in the air on each side of Noah's face. Despite unrestricted social contact being permitted amongst family members, it was still frowned upon.

"I'll be much better after a nice cup of hot coffee," Noah said and yawned. He grabbed a pair of latex gloves from the box on the counter and fitted his hands into them. Then, using a disinfectant wipe, he cleaned the bar stool and white marble top of the kitchen island where he sat each morning. "Where's Dad?"

"He'll be down soon. He's got that big meeting today with the partners at the clinic," Jasmine said. "They're looking at finally closing that deal on their new subscription-based Distance Band application."

"Oh, right. He's been obsessing about it for months."

"He's going to completely transform the landscape of medicine, giving patients the power to track their health data in real-time," Jasmine said. "But I hope his product is exactly what OWN Industries is looking for. I've heard their investors and agents can be poisonous." She started biting her nails as if she were the one selling it to OWN.

"He'll do great. Dad always comes through with things like this."

She gave him a half-hearted smile, but continued to chew at her nails. "Noah, you better order your breakfast on the tablet if you want it delivered before class starts. You've got to stay energized."

As if on cue, his stomach grumbled.

Jasmine turned away with her coffee, rummaging through a drawer. "Oh, and did you take your antidepressant?" she said as she opened her bottle and swallowed her pill.

Chapter Two

Noah sat at the kitchen island all morning, with his sleek silver phone flat on the surface next to him. Jasmine left for work at her husband's Mediclinic just before class started at nine. She'd landed the pharmacy position there three years ago, at the same time she'd met Noah's dad, Dr. Eamon Teslow.

Noah knew Eamon had never really come to terms with the untimely death of his first wife—and Noah's mom—Olivia, but the guilt had eased up over the years. He'd drowned out his thoughts with work and patients, but eventually, with Noah's "permission", he'd allowed himself to fall in love with his beautiful pharmacist, Jasmine. After a year-long engagement, they'd married in C47+, which had required a complicated authentication protocol of adding a new family member to their Distance Bands and household.

Noah's phone buzzed and a notification popped up, inviting him to attend his lecture. He grabbed his white bubble helmet from the counter and put it on. Its crystal blue visor slid down over his eyes. The technology was termed *Hover* and when Noah clicked the "Accept" button on his phone, the helmet emitted a light white glow to indicate it was ready for use. Hover had a two-way audio program for professors and students to communicate. The visor contained high-resolution screens that showed a VR view of the lecture room in the university with a 220-degree field of view.

He looked around the classroom. He was seated in the front row facing the stage where the lecturer stood. Other students were sitting all around him while others were just logging in at their pre-designated desks. As a reminder of real-world social distancing, the virtual desks were six feet apart horizontally and two rows apart vertically.

The Physiology professor, Dr. Rawlings, materialized on the stage, and the hubbub of conversation died away. He was transparent and light blue, like everybody else in the virtual space, but he wore waist-high dress pants and a button-up shirt enlivened with coffee spills. He paced constantly while lecturing, with a sloshing coffee mug in his hand. His wide glasses couldn't conceal his chronically-fatigued eyes.

"Good morning class, so sorry I was running late." He took a large swig from his mug and coughed. "I forgot to plug in my Hover helmet overnight and it died again. Nevertheless, here I am now, ready to bestow the foundations of Physiology upon the next generation of doctors and scientists."

Noah slumped on the kitchen stool at home as the lecture began, his chin resting on a chin-prop. Chin-props were one of the more popular student accessories, allowing the terminally bored to prop up their heads on a convenient flat surface. Professors weren't oblivious to the fact that students naturally lost interest over the course of a school day, no matter how stimulating they thought their lectures were. From Dr. Rawlings' perspective, he would have seen a sea of students seated with heads perched, some fighting to stay awake out of respect while others were out like a light, not even trying to feign interest.

Chin-props were just one of several items marketed in response to proper COVID etiquette; it was drilled into Noah at a very young age never to touch his face. "Your hands are the dirtiest things you could ever put to your face, Noah," his mom Olivia used to say. "You don't want to catch the variant, do you?" And that was the end of that. Noah's grandpa John loved to compare face touching of modern times to the nose picking of his time—both very much frowned upon, and both very much would get you a (gloved) smack.

"So, to finish up our lecture, would anyone care to tell me what determines cardiac output? This is for bonus marks," Dr. Rawlings said enthusiastically.

"I know professor!" Artemis Middlebrook cried from next to Noah in the front row, his right arm waving through the air. No one else seemed to care what the answer was. "Cardiac output is determined by heart rate multiplied by stroke volume. Now, if you want me to break it down even further, stroke volume is made up of end diastolic volume minus end systolic volume." Artemis grinned, the freckles of his smug face evident even on a transparent hologram. Noah rolled his eyes.

Kiss ass, he thought.

"Very good, Artemis," Dr. Rawlings said. "An extra two percent onto your final mark. You've been studying, I see, which will serve you well in your approaching finals. I hope the rest of you have been doing the same. For next class, I want everyone to read up on the beginnings of epinephrine research and discovery, dating all the way back to C124–. I think you'll find it *very* interesting. This can be found on pages 257-264 of your textbook. Next week, we will warp-speed ahead to modern physiology where our bodies function less and less by evolutionary processes and instead, intertwine with current technological and pharmacological means, thus altering our genetic make-up and transforming us to our meta-physiological state. More to come on this controversial matter. Thank you and enjoy the rest of your day." He vanished with the click of a button on the side of his Hover helmet.

Noah glanced around the class and saw that other students had beaten the professor to logging out. The room was already half-empty and dwindling by the second. Noah pressed the button to log out himself.

"Sounds like an interesting class," a voice in the real world said.

Noah jolted upright and cranked his neck around. *Ouch,* he thought as he rubbed the pulled muscle on his neck. His dad stood behind him, dressed up in a white shirt, black tie, and sharp grey suit. Even his horn-rimmed glasses and combed over hair were black, making Noah think more of an undertaker than a top-flight physician.

"Happy eighteenth, son," he said and ruffled Noah's unkempt hair with a gloved hand. "I got you something special this year."

He pulled a black velvet box from his pocket and put it on the counter. It was small enough to fit into the palm of his hand.

"You can open it later. I have to get going, but I'll be home by curfew tonight. Definitely no later than six-thirty. Anything you want to do for your birthday?"

"I was thinking we could—" Noah started, but his father's phone started ringing.

Eamon gave an apologetic look and reached for his pocket. "One second. I have to take this." Eamon turned around and said, "Hi, Mister Geist. I'm doing good. Yes, I'll be heading into the office shortly. Sounds good, I'll call you then. Looking forward to finalizing the deal with you and your team. Bye for now." He hung up and turned back around. "Sorry, you were saying?"

"I was thinking we could visit Grandma Noelle and Grandpa John."

"Like we do every year on your birthday," Eamon said and smiled. But his smiled faded almost at once. "I don't think that's a good idea this year, son. There's a big snowstorm coming in this evening. Expected to last at least three days. One of the worst in years, apparently."

Noah slumped on his stool.

"Chat with your stepmother and figure out something else to do. We'll talk about it when I get back."

And with that, he was gone.

Noah was left staring blankly at the door.

Chapter Three

Noah was dumbfounded by the brief conversation with his father.

Are we really going to let a snowstorm stop us? he thought.

His father knew that moments with Noah's grandparents were few and far between. They were getting older and Noah sensed he had only a few more opportunities to see them. But he pushed the thoughts away for now and picked up the light black gift box.

Birthday gifts were an uncommon custom in the C+ era. Families were more inclined to spend cherished moments together rather than spend money on gifts. Shortly before his ninth birthday, Noah remembered seeing an old movie on TV. It showcased a family of six seated around a table with a candle-lit cake as they sang "Happy birthday". He was awestruck at seeing children showered so merrily in gifts. When his birthday arrived that year, Noah pressed his grandparents about why he never received any gift and they'd laughed hysterically inside their pod.

"I'm sorry, dear," Grandma Noelle said, wiping a happy tear away. "It's just been so long since we heard someone ask something so innocent. No one exchanges gifts anymore, not since COVID arrived so unexpectedly on our shores from China."

"China," Grandpa John said. "The punchbag of the modern age. The world blames China for conceiving that wretched coronavirus and part of me doesn't blame the G-7 for their sanctions, either. If the Chinese government had been more transparent from the beginning, perhaps we could have put a lid on it before it transformed into this eternal pandemic."

Noah walked up to the glass barrier shielding his grandparents from him. "Grandpa, how was life for you guys in the C-Minuses? Before the pandemic?"

"Back in my day, we didn't use a ridiculous dating system with pluses and minuses, for a start. I was born in 1990, not C29–, like the government tries to tell me. The thought of dates based on the birth of COVID in 2019 . . . it sickens me."

"Don't let his grouchiness ruin your birthday, dear," Grandma Noelle said from her chair and winked. "Your grandfather is tired of hearing about COVID. And as if that wasn't enough, we've needed to safeguard against its deadly variants over the years. We thought COVID-25 was bad, but here we are with the COVID-37 mutation, which is even worse. It's all we've talked about for half our lives, ever since C0+."

"Could you stop referring to the years that way? It's like you've submitted to the government's decision on the matter! The year is 2060, NOT C40+," Grandpa John said.

"Whatever you say, dear," she said and rolled her eyes.

"The only good thing to come out of this whole COVID pandemic," Grandpa John said as he wagged his finger, "is that when we were forced to self-isolate, it proved how little we need to survive. Materialism overconsumed my generation—always buying the next best thing to chase a happiness that could never be reached. The irony still stings. It was only when consumerism went extinct that we realized human connection was the key to happiness. The eternal pandemic brought lockdowns, restricted gatherings, enforced two-meter social distancing, and more. Human connection—which we just took for granted—was taken away from us by law. Permanently."

Although Noah enjoyed the stories his grandfather told, no matter how gloomy they were at times, he wasn't bothered by how life used to be. Those of the End-Generation—like his grandparents—were of a different time.

After all, Noah was born post-COVID-19. This was the only life he knew.

He pulled himself back into the present and examined the gift in his hand. Gold trimming ran all the way around the middle of the box, ending at the hinges. Noah pried the box open as gently as he could.

Inside, on a cushion of white satin, an ancient relic lay, a piece of jewellery to invoke fear and confusion in anyone who saw it.

The symbol of The Cross.

Like every other household, Noah and his family were atheists. Which made this such a peculiar gift.

The Cross, given to him by his atheist dad.

What was he to do with it?

Chapter Four

Just before five o' clock, Noah heard the automated lock of the front door beeping and saw Jasmine enter. Exhaustion seeped from her skin.

"Hi, honey," she said as she came into the kitchen. "How was school today?" She set her purse on the counter next to the oven and bent forward to get a full bottle of red wine from the rack beside it.

"Boring. As usual," he said. He suddenly realized he'd left the cross on the counter and he snatched it up and hid it in his pants pocket.

Jasmine didn't seem to notice. "Do you want some Merlot?" she asked as she placed the wine bottle under an automated corkscrew set into the kitchen wall underneath the microwave. The device made a whizzing sound as it popped the cork off. Jasmine poured a generous amount of wine into a glass. She raised an eyebrow.

"Sure, why not," Noah said. "Long day at work?"

She poured another glass and carefully slid it across the counter to him.

"Long day would be an understatement," she said and gulped her wine. "Our main pharmaceutical distributor told us today we have a nation-wide shortage of Glyziga, which is unavailable until further notice. Of course, that led to a lot of angry phone calls from patients asking what they would do without their diabetes medication. Our pharmacy team was on damage control, but we survived." She lifted her wine glass with an air of annoyance.

"It can't be easy being an essential worker," Noah said. "Your work is important, Jasmine. We're lucky to live in an age when medicine can cure most illnesses."

"Doesn't feel like it, sometimes. Charles Darwin would be rolling in his grave. Natural selection is obsolete, thanks to the advancements in modern medicine. You'd think people would be more appreciative of what they have." She clenched her jaw. "Most people haven't got a clue what 'survival of the fittest' means. Not the way I did, living day-to-day on the streets. Anyway, it's not about that anymore. 'Survival of the richest' is more like it."

Jasmine rarely let her feelings out of the bottle, and Noah had seen it only a handful of occasions. She seemed to sense his uneasiness, because she smiled and said, "Sorry, Noah. That's the wine talking." She sipped from her glass. "I should be thankful we live in an essential household. Not everyone is so fortunate." She stood up and drained her glass. "I'm going to lie down on the couch and watch the evening news, if you need me."

"Jasmine," Noah said as she turned away. "Are we really not going to visit my grandparents this year?" The thought had been chewing at him all day. "Dad said there's a huge snowstorm on its way but is it going to be *that* bad? Is that really going to stop us?"

She frowned and planted her elbows on the counter. "Your dad's right about the snowstorm. But I'm going to be honest with you. We got word from the staff at Villa Salud. There's been a vicious COVID-37 outbreak in the past month. They're struggling to get it under control. Numerous End-Generationers have died already. They don't want any visitors there, simple as that. I hate to be so blunt, but we have to do our part to keep them safe."

"Are they okay? Are they safe?" Noah pictured his grandparents trapped inside their pod with COVID-37 funneling through the tunnels. Despite the safety measures inside their long-term care facility, Grandma Noelle and Grandpa John despised being cooped up like prisoners.

"They're fine," Jasmine said. "Your dad's been speaking regularly with the manager at Villa Salud. John and Noelle are safe and well in their pod."

"They're getting older," Noah said. "I'm worried I won't have much more time to spend with them."

"We'll visit them when the time is right, okay?" she said sharply. "Now, come join me in the living room to watch some TV."

She headed out of the kitchen and Noah swung around in his stool. Something didn't feel right about the whole situation. Long-term care facilities for the End-Generation were the safest places you could be, but still, he was uneasy.

A month-long outbreak? he thought. *No way.*

The initial COVID-19 years saw some of the worst outbreaks in long-term care facilities, killing many residents and sparking outrage in the families left behind. Things had changed drastically since those terrible days, and facilities now had established outbreak protocols to eliminate—or at least reduce—the risks from the deadly COVID-37 mutation.

Noah sensed both Jasmine and Eamon weren't being entirely honest with him.

He wasn't sure what was going on.

But he intended to find out.

Chapter Five

Noah got off his stool and kicked his legs to get the blood flowing again. He'd come to a decision. He wasn't going to miss out on seeing Grandma Noelle and Grandpa John. After all, visits were permitted only once a year, on privileged occasions, and who knew how many years they had left. He'd been counting down the days and weeks to today, and he was eager to hear more of Grandpa John's stories about life before COVID. But Noah needed to make sure Jasmine didn't spot him and that he was out before his dad returned.

He went into the living room and joined Jasmine on the couch.

"There you are," she said. "Just in time to catch the last bit of the news."

The TV on the wall opposite the couch showed a young blonde news anchor with prominent cheekbones, who sternly reported on the recent capture of another Hacker. "The suspect," she said gravely, "is a fifty-two-year-old male who attended an underground COVID-37 event a week ago."

A picture appeared in the left-hand corner of the screen, next to the anchor's head. It showed a grizzly-looking man who looked far older than fifty-two, with wicked blood-shot eyes and an unkempt grey-black beard and hair.

The news anchor continued, "He, along with others at this illegal event, deliberately infected themselves with a COVID-37 injection serum obtained from the black market. At approximately 12:45 p.m., the Hacker made his way to the *Food for Less* grocery store on Broadway Avenue, where he removed his mask and deliberately coughed on other shoppers. The victims are now with public health officials, placed in a secure self-isolation facility, where they will remain for fourteen days. The Hacker was arrested at the scene and brought in for further questioning."

Noah tried hard to listen, but his attention was drawn to the anchor's eyes, which had a pearly, translucent gleam to them; it was hard to focus on anything else. A career in media was a competitive business, and some went so far as to get state-of-the-art eye surgery to gain an advantage. The surgery embedded a microchip in the optic nerves, which was connected to an external transmitter, allowing reporters to provide first-person video directly from their eyes. Viewers could watch situations unfold on their TVs or cellphones as if they were there themselves.

"At this time," the anchor went on, "it is uncertain how many other Hackers attended the COVID-37 Super-Spreader event, and how the suspect removed his Distance Band without alerting the authorities. We'll bring you more on this story as it develops, so stay tuned and stay safe."

The camera slowly backed away from her desk and heroic music cued the end of the segment.

"Disgusting. Absolutely disgusting," Jasmine said. "How can these Hackers try to purposely spread disease when so many of us have done our part to stay safe? They should be executed."

A commercial came on the TV, showing a well-groomed young man in a black pinstripe suit. "Are you tired of all the doom and gloom you get from regular news networks?" he said enthusiastically to the camera. "Well, I have the solution for you. Here at Joy News, we bring you only positive news stories from across the globe. For a limited time, you can subscribe to our channel for just nine dollars a month for the first six months. Visit our website or call us toll-free to sign up now. Remember, we're here to bring you *joy*!"

Noah's parents had always encouraged him to stay up-to-date with the news, but many others opted out and instead listened only to good news networks like Joy News. For many people, ignorance really was bliss.

One commercial followed another. The advertisements were tailored to the family, based on their collective search histories from the internet, delivering the most relevant content. Noah glanced at Jasmine who was starting to doze off.

Just a bit longer, he thought, *and I'll be able to make my escape.*

He grabbed the TV remote and flipped channels. On one of them, Gregoire Talbot was speaking from a podium outside his house. The Prime Minister presented himself to the nation at least once a day, updating the citizens of Canada on the country's status quo and its ongoing fight against COVID-37. There was never any news of breakthroughs but the message remained the same: *hope.*

Behind the PM, four trusted advisors stood at the usual two-meter distance, two on each side. They all wore masks and expensive suits. The man on the far left was a bald, albino man with small, round spectacles perched on his hooked nose. Snowflakes melted on his cheeks, seemingly under the glare of his crimson eyes. He wore a red leather trench coat and a fine pair of white gloves. Noah had seen him on countless other broadcasts, and whenever he had, the hairs on the back of his neck stood up with a shiver running through his body.

This man was OWN Industries' director of Canada, working at the federal level of government. Noah's father knew the man through work. His name was Walter Geist and Noah had heard Eamon speaking with him on the phone that morning about the new Distance Band health app.

Talbot, with his stoic demeanour, pierced the camera with his steel-grey eyes and said, "COVID-37 does not discriminate between old or young, rich or poor. We are all on an *equal* battlefield when it comes to survival." His voice was powerful but husky. It was a voice that inspired confidence, trust, and a tremor of intimidation.

"However," he went on, "the people of Canada are resilient and enduring. Our country has some of the greatest minds in the world and with continued financial support into our science and research sector, I know we *will* finally find a vaccine to eradicate this fatal variant strain once and for all. I dream of a world in which we can truly have freedom, as our not-so-distant ancestors had. For now, do your part: keep six feet distance, wash your hands, and wear your mask. Goodnight to you all."

Talbot bowed with a hand over his chest, turned around, and left the podium. As the Prime Minister walked back into his house, the Canadian flag washed over the TV screen and the national anthem played. Noah glanced at Jasmine—she was slumped over the arm of the couch, snoring. Talbot's daily speeches were enough to knock anyone out.

Time to go, he told himself.

He rose carefully and crept toward the front door. When he got there, Jasmine was still snoring. To enter and exit the house, an authorized Distance Band was required, which was authenticated by the house's security system. Noah flashed his right wrist against the scanner above the door handle, which read the band locked on his arm. The door beeped softly and the light flashed green, sliding the door open to access the Disinfectant Chamber.

All the houses in wealthier neighbourhoods had a Disinfectant Chamber. It was sandwiched between the interior exit and the door leading to the outside world, like an airlock in a sci-fi spaceship. It was also the only port in and out of the property.

Noah entered the tall chamber, a closed rectangular space. He grabbed a pair of goggles from a shelf and put them on, adjusting them to fit snugly. There were several showerheads all around the room and when Noah pressed the glowing red button on the wall to his left, the showerheads squealed to life, spraying jets of disinfectant. Despite the goggles, he still closed his eyes as the cold mist sterilized him from head to toe. When the jets shut off, he removed the goggles and opened the closet next to the shelf.

Inside, there were several pre-sterilized, tight-fitting latex HAZMAT suits. They were white with light blue lining. Noah grabbed one from a metal hanger and put it on. His shoes fit into the bottom inserts of the suit and his hands fit into the gloves on the ends of the sleeves. He pulled the hood over his head, so only the oval of his face was uncovered.

The suit's left breast was printed with the logo of OWN Industries. The One World Network didn't just specialize in Distance Bands; they were one of the largest companies of the COVID-era, distributing HAZMAT suits, facemasks, goggles, hand sanitizers, and all kinds of other health and safety products. One by one, the letters of the logo lit up with light blue lighting. When it was fully illuminated, the suit tightened against his body like a second skin, but despite its close fit, Noah could breathe normally and move his limbs without restriction. The suit was covered in fine micro-pores, invisible to the naked eye, but allowing the exchange of oxygen and carbon dioxide with each breath, without accumulating one or the other. It was designed to prevent any viral, bacterial, or fungal organisms from entering the pores, simply filtering them based on their size.

The last piece of the suit was the helmet and a row of them sat on the shelf underneath the suits, like the severed heads of robots. Each had a thick, black inverted triangular face-shield with the edges rounded out, extending from temples to chin. They weighed almost nothing. Noah grabbed one and flipped the face-shield up before placing it over his head. It instantly cast a magnetic buffer around his skull; the face-shield slid down an inch in front of his face, sealing with the edges of the suit's hood.

This is what being a member of an essential household gets you, he thought. *Top grade protection from the outside world.*

Noah often felt claustrophobic wearing his suit and he took a few deep breaths to calm himself and adjust to the constriction. The face-shield briefly fogged up before the humidity inside the suit stabilized at the correct level and the inside of the visor lit up with yellow digital readings at the top left. Noah's vital signs—from heart rate and blood pressure to oxygen saturation—were all displayed and looked normal, though his heart was racing. The top right displayed an external temperature reading of −15 Celsius and the current time of 5:45 p.m.

"No turning back now," he whispered to himself and tapped his Distance Band against the scanner on the exterior door. It beeped, the light flashed green, and the door slid open. He stepped onto the front porch with the door behind him locking shut. Noah stood frozen for a moment, gazing up at a twilight sky painted with bruised purple and blue and gently falling snow.

"I'll be back, Jasmine. I promise," he said to the empty wind.

Then he was off.

Chapter Six

Noah stepped down from the porch. His feet crunched in the snow and left oval footprints behind from the HAZMAT suit. Jasmine's silver Tesla was parked in the driveway and Noah held up his wrist to the driver's door, which beeped and unlocked. He climbed into the car and settled into the comfortable leather seat as the pressure-activated heating hummed. The seatbelts automatically buckled him in. Charles, the ubiquitous AI voice of the Teslow's audio systems, awoke.

"Good evening, Noah," he said. "Where would you like to go today?"

Why do these companies always go for a British accent? Noah thought. In old movies, British accents were usually reserved for the bad guys.

The digital dashboard displayed the same question, and Noah said, "Villa Salud, Charles."

"Very good, sir," Charles said, and the engine purred into life.

The Tesla reversed slowly out of the driveway. Every vehicle built in the last fifteen years was carbon-neutral, voice-controlled, and self-driven. As Noah relaxed into the driver's seat, he tuned in to the soft elevator music playing in the background. A map on the dashboard indicated his location with a pulsing white circle.

"You have twenty-one minutes before arriving at your destination," Charles said serenely. "Is there anything you would like to amuse yourself with? I can pull up your social media accounts, or an episode of *All in this Together*. You left off at season four, episode five, and it has been two days since you last watched."

"I'll keep the music for now, Charles. I need some space to think." Noah was picturing what he would say to his grandparents; he hadn't seen them for a year. But a little voice at the back of his mind kept prodding him with the same questions:

Was there truly an outbreak at Villa Salud? Am I jeopardizing my family by leaving so close to curfew? What will the police do—or, more importantly, what will my parents *do to me? Should I turn back now, before it's too late?*

As his mind raced, he peered at the houses on his block as he passed them. They were all precisely the same size, color, and build. To his left, a front-facing window had partly-open curtains and a hunched, bald man was trying unsuccessfully to conceal himself behind them. He stared intently at the Tesla as it passed, and Noah could see the bright light of the phone in his hands. The man scowled then tapped the phone's screen before turning his back to the window, swallowed by the darkness of his living room.

As the Tesla drove past the next house, Noah noticed another person by their window, a woman with thick curly hair and dark circles under her eyes. She too spun away and disappeared into the darkness, a phone in her hand. He found himself watched from house after house, and as the car picked up speed, his pulse pounded in his ears and on his face-shield's display.

"Vitals off!" Noah said and the digits vanished from his peripheral vision. Watching his heart rate climb to 140 bpm heightened an unfamiliar anxiety in him.

I should've known better than to sneak off at this hour, when the entire neighbourhood would notice, he thought.

The car took a right turn onto the main road. His tension eased now that the Neighbourhood Watch was behind him. He sighed and shut his eyes for a moment.

I hope this is worth it.

As the minutes ticked by, the snowfall grew heavier. The vehicle's windshield wipers automatically cleared it at an appropriate pace but the more distance he put between himself and his home, the worse the road's visibility became. Nevertheless, the car turned onto the freeway and accelerated to cruising speed. Saskatoon was small enough to drive from one end of the city to the other in thirty minutes.

As he sailed toward Villa Salud, Noah thought about a previous visit to see his grandparents, on his seventh birthday.

*

His grandparents had seemed to be in the middle of an argument within their pod when he arrived with his mom and dad. But as soon as he appeared, the tension evaporated and his grandparents beamed at him.

"I've been waiting all day for you, my boy," Grandpa John said, as he eased himself into his chair. "I was afraid you wouldn't show up this year."

"Your grandpa's been making me dizzy," Grandma Noelle said. "Watching him do loops around the pod. Thank goodness you saved me from this pitiful boredom."

"I've missed you both so much!" Noah cried. "Tell me a story, like you always do, Grandpa." He ran up to the glass barrier separating him from his grandparents.

Eamon and Olivia Teslow waved to John and Noelle before seating themselves on the couch, letting Noah absorb all the attention from his grandparents.

"Do I have a history lesson for you, my boy," Grandpa John said. "I want you to know what life was like before the pandemic, how it's meant to be lived. But as always, keep it hush-hush, you hear? There's no telling the trouble we'd get into for discussing these topics every year, but

God knows, school isn't going to teach you these things." He winked and Noah's dad nodded grudgingly, though he was smiling.

"Tell him about the planes, dear," Grandma Noelle said. "He'll love that."

Noah gawked at them and sat cross-legged on the cold tile floor in front of the glass.

Grandpa John stroked his chin. "You know those police drones you see flying around from time to time?"

"I love seeing them fly by our house," Noah said.

"Hm. Well, imagine a drone so big it could carry a hundred people inside it—or five hundred—and fly anywhere in the world!" Grandpa John expanded his arms in a wide circle. "Your grandma and I used to fly in those big metal birds. We flew to our second home in San Diego, to see your grandma's family. That was before they closed the borders, of course."

Grandma Noelle's face fell. "Halfway through C1+—"

"You mean mid-2020," Grandpa John corrected her.

She scowled at him and said, "Halfway through C1+, the government called for further measures to restrict travel between countries. The airlines companies folded and all those big metal birds went into hibernation. The risk of bringing COVID-19 back to home soil was too high of a risk for any country. Not only did borders between countries close, but so too did the borders between provinces in Canada— permanently."

Grandpa John sighed loudly. "Boy, do I miss escaping the cold and sitting on a warm Mexican beach with a margarita in my hand. Not that the cold matters now. We're stuck in this godforsaken place all year round."

"Dad," Eamon said. "Count yourself lucky you're here. Not every End-Generationer is fortunate enough to receive a retirement package inside a top-grade long-term care facility."

"This ain't retirement, it's a death sentence. If I'd known this would be our little prize from the government for surviving past sixty-five, I would've kept working. At least that way I'd feel useful. I gave the best years of my life to the frontlines of healthcare."

"Honey, please," Grandma Noelle said. "You'll get your blood pressure up again."

"What's an End-Generationer?" Noah asked.

Grandpa John got up from his chair and limped to the glass barrier. He crouched down to meet Noah at eye level. "We are the last of a special breed, the ones who knew life before the pandemic. The few who survived the devastation of COVID-19 and its fatal variants."

*

The Tesla drove down Circle Drive's main road, which housed many of the city's businesses. It passed Eamon's clinic, a mammoth, grey concrete building eight stories high, occupying most of the business block over which it towered. Despite the drifting snow, the clinic's two-meter-high neon sign shone brightly.

The vehicle stopped at a red traffic light. Noah checked the dashboard for the time and saw it was just after six. As if reading Noah's mind, Charles said, "Four more minutes until you reach Villa Salud." Noah craned his neck forward, trying to make out the road ahead, but the view was dense with swirling snow.

Noah was nearing the outskirts of Saskatoon. The Tesla drove along a stretch of road deeply packed with snow; a meridian strip lined with bare trees separated the two opposing lanes going into and out of Villa Salud. A snow-covered sign stood at the facility's entranceway:

Welcome to Villa Salud. We wish you a pleasant visit with your loved ones. As always, stay safe.

As he passed the sign, a chill ran through Noah's body. The vehicle slowed. Ahead of him, he saw the glow of the facility's large bubble dome of transparent glass; the light from within brilliantly illuminated the spiraling snow and the twilight sky. As he neared it, a security kiosk's long hinged barrier blocked the road and a steel roller door guarded the entrance into the parkade.

"Charles," Noah said, "lower the window for me, please."

"As you wish, sir."

At once, the driver's window lowered and a flurry of snow rushed into the vehicle. Noah reached out and pressed his right wrist against the security kiosk's pressure pad. The machine authenticated his Distance

Band, verifying that he had family within Villa Salud. He pulled his arm back inside and the window rose automatically. The barrier swung up and the car moved forward as the roller door slid up smoothly and silently. Light from inside the parkade flooded the snow-covered road and the car's tires crunched slowly ahead.

As the Tesla's front bumper entered the parkade, an exit door opened on the other side of the median. Noah's heart sank as he watched a black Tesla SUV leave the parkade. Through the window, he caught a glimpse of the other driver, a man in a white HAZMAT suit with light blue lining.

Noah's father drove slowly out of Villa Salud.

Chapter Seven

Noah sat rigid with disbelief. He gripped the steering wheel tightly. Why had his dad told him to stay home while he saw fit to visit Grandpa John and Grandma Noelle himself?

Hypocrite, he thought. *Damn hypocrite. He knows how important this day is to our family. To me.*

Thankfully, Eamon hadn't noticed Noah driving in.

"You have now arrived at your destination, Noah," Charles said gallantly. "I trust the ride was to your liking, despite the weather."

"Yeah," Noah said. "It was just great." He rolled his eyes; even the software wanted validation.

He had no idea what was going on in here. Was there really a COVID-37 outbreak or was Jasmine lying to him? If there was an outbreak, why would his dad risk his grandparents'—and his own—health to come here?

He stepped out of the vehicle and glanced around the parkade. It was a massive lot but there wasn't a single other vehicle in sight, which raised more questions. He'd have expected to see a couple more visitors leaving at this hour. Perhaps it was the blizzard keeping them home.

Noah walked toward the entrance, which led into the atrium of Villa Salud. The automated doors sighed softly as they parted. Inside the atrium, he marvelled at the beauty of this facility. In the center, a large pine tree stood, fifty feet high, bejeweled with bright white lights and multi-colored ornaments, topped with a gold star. It was just inches short of the dome's apex. There was a little wooden fence around the tree's base and the white marble floors reflected the light from twirling chandeliers above.

Noah examined the ornaments. Each one housed a picture of an End-Generationer who'd lost their lives to COVID-19 and its variants, along with their birth and death dates. The pictures changed every thirty seconds to show a new person. As the faces rotated, the silence of the facility pricked Noah's senses; not a single soul was in sight, resident or staff.

Wouldn't there be hysteria in here if an outbreak really were taking place?

At the far end of the atrium, there was a digital board high up on the glass wall and Noah hurried up to it. As he stared up at the screen, hundreds of floating bubbles bounced around the display. Each bubble contained the contact information of a Villa Salud resident. Noah struggled to find his grandparents among the moving targets.

"John and Noelle Teslow!" Noah shouted at the screen.

A bubble at the bottom left corner expanded, popping all the others as it ballooned to fill the whole screen. It contained his grandparent's names, along with their tunnel and pod number.

John and Noelle Teslow: #6—618.

Individuals and couples were housed in glass pods, branching off from various tunnels, with the atrium at the hub. Although he came here every year, Noah always felt like he was in a maze. He turned in a slow circle, trying to identify Tunnel 6. Finally, he spotted a wide door inscribed with the number 6 in shiny gold and he jogged to it.

Almost there, he thought.

He pressed his right wrist against the lock pad beside the door and his Distance Band granted authorization. The metal door hissed up and Noah entered Tunnel 6. The door descended behind him, sealing him in. The tunnel was about twenty feet wide and brightly lit, with two parallel paths for visitors to come and go. There was a faint beeping in the distance. Noah climbed one step up onto the right-hand side walkway which was at a standstill.

"Pod six-one-eight," he said.

The walkway automatically hummed to life, propelling him forward at a little more than walking pace. As he traversed through the tunnel passing multiple disembarking points, the beeping grew louder. He held onto the handrail and peered out through the glass walls, but he could see nothing but snowfall; the blizzard pressed against the glass tunnel as if begging to enter. He wondered how his dad was managing the drive home. And how he'd manage himself, later.

The walkway slowed as it neared Pod 618 on the right-hand side. Noah stepped off the disembarking point and hurried to another door which opened as he approached. He entered a short passageway that expanded into a bay—a visiting room for family with couches and chairs. His grandparents' pod was separated from the visiting room by a thick glass wall from floor to ceiling. Despite the need to protect End-Generationers this way, Noah couldn't help but think of animals caged in a zoo.

Noah took a deep breath as he approached the pod. The beeping was coming from in here somewhere, loud enough to make his ears ring.

"Grandma, Grandpa!" he called. "It's Noah. I came by to surprise you. My parents told me not to visit, but I just couldn't pass up the opportunity to see both of you—"

He stopped short. Beyond the glass wall, he saw his grandparents in their comfortable pod. But both were slumped forward in their leather chairs, IV lines running from their arms to bags hanging from metal stands. They were both connected to loudly beeping machines.

"What the—" Noah cried. "Let me help you!" He banged on the glass, which reverberated dully. "Is there a way to get in?"

Grandpa John raised his head slowly and looked at Noah with tired eyes. Beads of sweat dotted his paper-thin skin. He managed to produce a soft smile. He appeared so much older than last year; even with his cap on, it was obvious his grey hair had thinned and his clothes hung loosely on his body.

"My dear boy," he said, his voice resembling dying embers in a fire. "I'm so sorry you had to see us this way. We've been sick for a while, from isolation and despair. We've lived this long, but the world isn't what it used to be, what it could've been for us . . . and for you. Our time is up, I'm afraid."

"What are you saying?" Noah said. His eyes were suddenly wet. "When did you get sick? I can find someone to help, just please tell me what's happened."

"It will all be explained in due time, my dear boy, trust me. My sweet Noelle has already left this world. She always beat me to the punch in everything, even into the afterlife." He laughed weakly until it turned into a coughing fit. He covered his mouth with a handkerchief, but Noah spotted the blood-stained sputum he produced. "We'll meet again soon, that I know." He sat back in his chair and let out one last breath.

Noah stood with his hand on the glass and tears on his face. Two inches of glass separated him from his grandparents but in that moment, they were worlds apart. The beeping of the machinery abruptly stopped and Noah heard a voice behind him.

"I told you not to come here tonight, Noah. You should've listened."

He spun around. His father stood behind him in his HAZMAT suit. In his right hand, he held a sledgehammer, which swung lazily against the side of his leg.

"Dad! Grandma and Grandpa are dead. We have to get in there. I found them hooked up to all sorts of equipment. Who would do something like this?"

"Noah, you really shouldn't have snuck out like that," Eamon said. "There's going to be a big change of plans now. I'll have to take matters into my own hands."

He strode straight at Noah, his face flashing fury. He drew the sledgehammer back above his shoulder.

Noah closed his eyes and covered his face with both hands.

His father swung the sledgehammer down upon him.

Chapter Eight

Noah heard the smash of safety glass shattering and gummy chunks of it showered his suit, pinging off his face-shield. He still had his hands raised, as if they'd protect him from a thundering sledgehammer. He slowly opened his eyes and looked up at his dad.

"I thought you were going to kill me!"

Eamon frowned at him. "What are you talking about?" he said and poked the hole he'd just created in the glass wall, widening it. Fragments pattered onto the floor. "Noah, I know you've got a lot of questions, but we don't have much time right now." He brushed past Noah and stepped carefully into the pod. "We're in danger."

"In danger? Who from?" Noah said. "How did you know I was here?"

"I didn't," Eamon said. "I made an educated guess. I was on my way home when I saw a fleet of police drones flying toward here. I couldn't be certain you were involved, but I figured if there was a call heading that way during a blizzard, it might have something to do with a certain birthday boy missing his grandparents so much he'd do whatever it took to see them."

Noah flushed. "Police drones are on their way?"

"Oh, you thought you could leave home unnoticed, without a thousand eyes watching you like a hawk? The Neighbourhood Watch is always alert. You should have known better, Noah."

Noah was silent for a moment. "I'm sorry," he said eventually. "I just couldn't imagine waiting another year to see them. But you know what? I'm glad I did it, because I got to speak with Grandpa one last time. Before . . ." He choked back the tears this time. "What happened to them?"

Eamon slowly crossed the pod and leaned over Grandpa John to remove something from around his neck. "They've been in here a long time, Noah. Sure, safety from COVID-37 is one thing, but their quality of life wasn't great." He turned to Grandma Noelle and looked sadly down at her. "They asked me to help."

"Help with what?"

"Medical assistance. To help them die."

"And you agreed?" Noah clenched his fists and walked up to the hole in the barrier.

Eamon turned his back and stooped over Grandma Noelle, removing something from around her neck too. He then sprayed the objects with sanitizer from a tiny canister on his wrist and placed them in a pocket of his HAZMAT suit.

"I didn't agree, not at first," Eamon said and turned to face Noah. His eyes were blank. "I couldn't even contemplate doing something like that. But over time, well they convinced me. You know what Grandpa John is . . . was . . . like. I told them about the work I was involved with and they devised a plan to help me. They were ready to move on, but they didn't want to die in vain." He looked at Noah with a sudden mixture of defiance and pain. "As I said, we don't have much time. The police are on their way."

In the distance, Noah heard the blaring of police sirens from somewhere in the network of tunnels. Their bodies stiffened like boards. No matter what kind of influence his dad had in the community, there would be major repercussions for Noah violating curfew.

Why didn't I just stay home? he thought miserably.

"We need to go now," Eamon said and clambered out of the pod.

He grabbed Noah by the elbow and dropped the sledgehammer among the chunks of glass. They ran back toward the narrow passageway leading into the tunnel. The sirens were louder, almost deafening. As Noah followed his dad into the tunnel, he saw flashes of blue and red reflecting from the glass walls to their left.

His father led him across the tunnel and onto the exit route walkway. It immediately hummed to life.

"Lie down," Eamon said. "We're going for a ride." He reached the handrail and configured something on the interface.

Noah and Eamon dropped flat onto their backs. Everything about today was completely upside down. This was not the birthday Noah had had in mind.

The walkway sped up well over its default pace, shooting them down the tunnel toward the atrium. High above, seven black and white drones shot past them, each the size of a big screen TV, their four razor-sharp propellers slicing the air. The tunnel was awash with red and blue lights and deafening sirens. Noah glimpsed the cameras on the underside of each machine. And the array of weapons.

Seven lenses swiveled toward him, and the drones slowed.

Seven sets of artillery barrels pointed directly at him.

Chapter Nine

As the drones readied their weapons, Noah and Eamon reached the Tunnel 6 exit. They jumped to their feet, scrambled off the walkway, and ran to the metal door. Momentum carried the drones down the tunnel. Noah thrust his wrist against the sensor on the wall and the door slid open. The pair sprinted into the atrium, where the great pine tree glimmered in the middle of the dome.

"We've got to keep moving," Eamon said and headed for the tree. "Charles, call Justus Okenawah and add Noah Teslow to the call."

Noah knew Justus was the manager at Villa Salud and a lifelong friend of his father, who'd helped Justus get the job years ago.

"Calling Justus Okenawah and Noah Teslow," Charles said calmly.

There was a brief pause, then a voice said, "Hello, my friend." Noah heard Justus clearly through his HAZMAT suit's speakers. "I was just about to have a cup of tea." He sighed. "I imagine that'll have to wait, based on what I can see on the security screen here."

"I'm sorry, Justus," Eamon said. "The wheels are now in motion but not in the way we intended, I'm afraid. My son and I need your help to get out of here. Anything you can do?"

Justus answered immediately and without questions. "I'll lock the Tunnel 6 door. It won't stop the drones for long—they're too well-equipped—but it'll give you a little more time to make your escape."

Noah and Eamon were halfway to the tree when they heard sharp screeches beyond the Tunnel 6 door—the sound of metal on metal as a couple of the drones tested the door. Noah glanced back and saw red points of light precisely tracing the outline of the door, spewing a cascade of sparks. The points met at the top of the doorframe and the door fell forward, clanging onto the marble floor. The noise was deafening, and Noah watched as the swarm of drones rushed out.

"Any other thoughts there, Justus?" Eamon said. "We're, ah, a bit pressed for time here."

"We order you to stop immediately." The drones spoke in unison, seven robotic voices amplified by the atrium's dome. The sirens and lights blared on and Noah could feel the wind from their propellers. "You have been deemed a threat to public safety," the drones said. "Raise your hands and lie face-down on the floor. If you do not comply, we are authorized to use force."

Noah and Eamon kept running, which was all it took to exhaust the drone's rudimentary patience. Noah's feet stumbled over themselves and he fell, as a short burst of automatic weapon fire zipped over his head, ricocheting off the marble and showering him with sharp chunks of stone. Eamon ducked and pulled Noah to his feet.

The atrium chandeliers and the tree lights went out. Noah's face-shield immediately converted to night-vision mode in the darkness. The gun fire ceased while the drones adapted their cameras. There was a sudden piercing wail, coming from the top of the tree and when Noah glanced behind, the drones were whirling in the air like dazed birds, their lenses focusing randomly.

Justus spoke through the suit's speakers. "You can thank the General for that one. His idea to install a service disrupter. It's coming from the star on top of the tree. It's disabled the drones long enough for you to get out. There's a hatch door at the base of the tree. I've unlocked it from here. On your way out, deactivate your phones so they can't be used to track you."

"Thank you, my friend," Eamon said, his voice cracking. "I don't know how I'll ever repay you."

"You've got a long road ahead of you, doc, and plenty of time to think about it. Good luck to you both," Justus said. "And goodbye."

The line went dead.

Chapter Ten

Noah and his father stared at each other in the darkness. As the drones continued to bumble about overhead, they jumped over the low fence and crawled under the tree. A large handle protruded from the floor near the base of the trunk and Noah crouched on the balls of his heels to pull it. The door lifted easily enough.

"You first, Dad."

Eamon gave a half-hearted smile and jumped into the hole. He clambered down the rungs of a ladder attached to the side. Noah followed and closed the hatch above him. As they descended, lights flicked on each step of the way. They climbed down at least fifty feet before they reached solid ground. Noah looked around and saw they were in another parking lot, this one completely packed with cars, the likes of which he had never seen before.

"They're old, huh?" Eamon said. "You won't find any of these at a dealership."

"Who drives these things?"

"They belong to the End-Generationers in Villa Salud. They sit here collecting dust while the residents live in the comfort of their pods."

"We're not taking our vehicles?" Noah asked. "They're still upstairs in that empty parking lot."

"Not a chance, son. They might as well have a target on their roofs. Drones would track us down in minutes. No, we've got to be more careful than that. Now, turn off your phone."

They walked down the aisles between the ancient cars and had Charles deactivate their phones.

"And there she is," Eamon said at last.

They stopped in front of a C1+ Jeep Grand Cherokee, a four-door SUV with a few scratches on its paintwork. Eamon drew a line with his finger in the dust on the car's hood.

"I hope this thing still has some juice left in it," he said and pulled a set of keys from a pocket of his suit. "I grabbed these from your grandparents' pod. I've got a plan to get us out of here safely."

"Where will we go?" Noah said. "How are we going to explain all this to Jasmine? Is she safe? Are the police waiting for us at home already?" Jasmine must be sick with worry by now.

"You've got plenty of questions," Eamon said. "You'll get answers soon enough."

His face clouded with regret and he walked around to the back of the car, where he lifted two jerry cans out of the trunk. He started pouring gasoline into the car's tank, something Noah had only ever read about in books; all vehicles made since C7+ were electric. The smell of the gas was pungent even through Noah's suit.

"Get in the car," Eamon said. "We'll talk as we drive."

Noah opened the passenger door and climbed in. He noticed that the seat didn't adjust to his pressure, nor automatically fasten his seatbelt. Charles didn't greet him and there were dozens of little dials and buttons on the dashboard.

Eamon sat in the driver's seat, put his foot on the brake pedal, and pressed the *Start* button. The vehicle lurched, as if angry to be stirred after years of slumber. Eamon pressed the button a couple more times and eventually, the Jeep's engine roared to life.

Eamon grabbed a handle between the front seats and switched the vehicle into reverse gear, using one hand on the steering wheel with the other on the back of Noah's seat as he craned his head around to look out the back window. He reversed smoothly out of the parking bay.

"Oh, and there's another thing that we need to take care of," he said.

He put the car back into *Park* briefly and patted the pockets of his suit. He eventually found what he was looking for and said, "Here it is."

He pulled out a thin, palm-sized object, shaped like a tiny horseshoe. "Give me your right arm," he said and grabbed Noah's wrist impatiently. He dropped the horseshoe over Noah's Distance Band, which sparked and crackled.

Noah stared at his wrist then looked up at his dad. "Have you gone completely mad?" he gasped and punched him in the arm. "You've disabled my Distance Band! You just gave me a death sentence!"

Eamon put the vehicle back into *Drive* and started toward the exit. "It's too much of a risk. We can be tracked through Distance Bands. And like I said, this is all part of my contingency plan."

"What contingency plan?" Noah shouted. Just what the hell was going on tonight?

Eamon glanced at Noah and looked away almost immediately. "Okay," he said. "You need to know, so I'll tell you." He took a deep breath. "I've been operating as a spy against OWN Industries, Noah."

"What?"

"You heard me."

"A spy? What are you talking about?"

They circled around the parkade, driving up ramps, rising toward the surface. "For the past three years or so, I've been working closely with trusted contacts involved in an underground initiative . . . with the goal of bringing down the One World Network."

"I don't understand," Noah said. "What exactly have you been doing?"

"You know that new technology I've been working on? A Distance Band application to continuously monitor blood sugar, cholesterol, cancer markers, and all the rest? Well, I do believe in its utility, but it was mostly a front for me to connect with OWN delegates." Eamon swung the car around another corner and up another ramp. "They wanted in as soon as they heard about it. They saw a profit, so they moved in. I've gotten to know many of their top guys over the last few years and bits of sensitive information slipped out from time to time." He gripped the steering wheel tightly. "The world has been manipulated for far too long."

They finally reached the exit. Eamon manually lowered the window on the driver's side and unbuckled his seatbelt. He pressed his wrist against the lock pad and the door slid open. Before pulling away, he disabled his Distance Band with the horseshoe device. "There," he said smirking as he refastened his seatbelt. "We're even now."

"And your meeting today?" Noah asked. "What happened there?"

"It didn't happen. Fell through at the last minute. I can't be certain, but I think I know why."

He drove out of the parkade and the car was immediately bombarded by a flurry of snow. The windshield wipers swatted at it, but visibility was more limited now than when Noah had arrived an hour and a half ago. Eamon drove for about half a kilometer then turned left onto a back road. The car crept along slowly, Eamon leaning forward over the steering wheel as if that would help him see any further.

The road ahead was deserted at this hour. But more importantly, there were no signs of police drones.

After what felt like an eternity of driving in silence, Noah asked, "Where are we going?"

Eamon glanced over at him and said, "Calgary."

"Calgary as in Calgary, Alberta? As in over the provincial border?"

"That's the one."

"You've got to be kidding me," Noah said. He shook his head. "So, we're just breaking all the rules, then. Maybe we could stop for a bit of armed robbery on the way. Or burn a couple of charity foundations down."

Eamon said, "Yeah, you're hilarious. Look, I contacted my associates in Calgary when I drove back to Villa Salud. They're expecting us later tonight."

"All part of the contingency plan, right?"

"Correct."

They reached the outskirts of Saskatoon and turned onto Highway 7 and its many tunnels, each one stretching for kilometers at a time. They both sighed with relief when they entered the first brightly-lit tunnel; at last, they could see the road clearly.

"Dad," Noah said at length. "I'm really sorry about all of this. I shouldn't have been so selfish. I should've just stayed home, like you said."

"It's not your fault, Noah. It's mine, I should've been more honest with you from the beginning. You'll meet a lot of new people in Calgary, who've been working diligently in silence. We'll soon have the key to escaping the chains of government control. The free world—the one your grandparents grew up in, before C0+—is within reach."

Behind them, Noah heard the roar of a revving engine. He twisted in his seat and stared out through the back window. A lone biker, dressed in an all-black HAZMAT suit, was rapidly approaching on a black motorcycle. It was a few hundred yards back, but gaining, and Eamon stamped on the gas pedal. Noah was pushed back in his seat and watched the speedometer on the dashboard rise to 200 kph. But the bike was faster and the gap was closing. Noah extended his neck again, but couldn't see the face of the rider behind a tinted black face-shield.

The bike drew alongside the Jeep and its rider produced a gun, pointing it directly at Eamon.

"Dad, look out!" Noah cried.

There were two loud, flat *cracks* and Eamon swerved across the lanes. The bike dropped back, but one bullet destroyed the left side-view mirror and another shattered the rear window. Freezing air rushed into the car and the noise of the wind was almost deafening. Eamon and Noah both slid down in their seats.

The bike drew level again and the rider pointed the gun at Eamon. He pulled the steering wheel left, bumping the bike, and the rider dropped the gun, which clattered away behind. The bike dropped back again.

Eamon gripped the steering wheel tightly and accelerated still more, weaving back and forth across the highway's lanes. They gained some distance as the rider struggled to regain control of the bike and stop it from wobbling.

"Hold on tight," Eamon said through clenched teeth.

Noah was jolted violently forward and his seatbelt snapped tight across his chest. The Jeep braked to a complete stop, tires squealing and smoke rising from them in blue clouds. Eamon wrestled with the steering wheel as it pulled to the left, threatening to fishtail. Various warning lights appeared on the dashboard and Noah felt his heart in his throat. There was a sudden lurch, which jolted the Jeep forward a couple of feet, and Noah twisted around in time to see the motorbike hit the rear bumper. The rider was catapulted over the Jeep's roof and slammed down onto the asphalt ahead, skidding twenty feet further down the road.

Noah stared at his father. Both of them were hyperventilating.

"Whoa," Noah said, trying to stop his hands from shaking.

Eamon inched the Jeep forward, navigating around the mangled, bloody body on the ground. The figure's black HAZMAT suit was torn to shreds and the tinted face-shield was cracked up the middle.

"Who is it?" Noah said, eyeing the body as they inched past it.

"Nobody good, that's for sure," Eamon said.

They picked up speed again, leaving the wreckage behind. As they drove off, Noah glanced back through the smashed window and saw their would-be assassin rise slowly, clutching their chest, hunched forward. The rider took off the black helmet and threw it to the ground.

Noah gasped as her jet-black hair fell around her face. Her olive-skin was swollen and bruised, and her hazel eyes were ringed with black.

Jasmine Teslow watched the Jeep accelerate away for a moment, then collapsed to the ground.

Noah plunged into complete darkness.

Chapter Eleven

Prime Minister Gregoire Talbot sat at his desk in his dark green leather chair, flipping through the agenda for the upcoming annual Climate Change Summit. His study was dimly lit and its walls were dressed with oil paintings of his predecessors, who watched his every move.

The wind howled against the windows, the panes of which were blocked by thick snow.

A gentle knock interrupted his focus. He put down his flexiglass tablet and peered at the door.

"For God's sake," he muttered. "Who is it?"

The heavy oak door creaked open, revealing a bespectacled bald man wearing a red leather trench coat.

"Ah, Mister Geist. Come in, come in "

"Sorry to interrupt you at this hour, Mister Prime Minister. But it's important." Geist pulled off his white gloves and sat in a chair on the other side of the broad desk.

"What news do you bring?" Geist's pale face was difficult to read at the best of times, but his crimson eyes were inscrutable.

"Our secret weapon, she has failed us," Geist said.

Talbot smacked his desk, then crossed his arms and sat silently for a moment. "Well? What happened?"

"There was an accident on the highway as she was pursuing the target. He got away."

"How bad is it?"

"Very." Geist leaned forward, listing off the injuries on his fingers. "Subdural brain bleed, bilateral pneumothorax, multiple broken ribs, ruptured spleen, and a broken jaw. She was practically dead at the scene."

Talbot unfolded his arms and clasped his hands on the desk. "And where is she now?"

"Taken by a medi-drone to the nearest hospital, sir."

"This is what happens when you put your trust in an ex-addict," Talbot snorted. "The irony isn't lost on me: you live on the street, you die on the street."

Walter Geist frowned and pulled his coat tighter around his slender frame. "Gregoire, she was the best of the best."

Talbot stared at Geist for a moment. The damn albino was getting ideas above his station, daring to address him by his first name. But he'd let it slide. This time.

"The best of the best? What are we paying you for if that's the best you've got? Let me remind you, OWN Industries would be nothing without my government's funding."

Geist stood up and slammed his fists on the desk. "And let me remind *you* that if it weren't for *your* government, my dear Ophelia would still be here today." He exhaled slowly and straightened his coat. He stood upright. "I apologize. That was out of line."

Talbot smirked. "Walter, I didn't take you for a sentimental man. As you yourself have told me countless times, she was a necessary means to an end. Should I be questioning your loyalty?"

"Of course not. I take my responsibilities very seriously and I'm committed to our mutual cause. My indoctrination practices are unbreakable, the training of our agents is unmatched. This evening was . . . an unexpected shortcoming."

Talbot stretched his neck slowly from side to side. "Yes, it was. Do everything you can to revive her, Walter. The priority remains the same— the General needs to be brought home."

"And if she is damaged beyond repair?"

Talbot picked up his flexiglass tablet and flipped through the agenda. "You know my orders. She won't be the first."

Walter Geist's crimson eyes brimmed with silent rage. "Anything for you, sir."

Chapter Twelve

Walter Geist marched through the encrmous factory. His red coat reflected dully in the charcoal grey epoxy flooring. He passed the colossal assembly lines that churned out OWN-manufactured products.

Wonderful, Geist thought.

The One World Network facility was in the heart of Ottawa. Walter Geist, one of the original founders of One World Network Industries, oversaw the operations in Canada. They were responsible for manufacturing and distributing pandemic products such as HAZMAT suits, Disinfectant Chambers, and Distance Bands.

Geist stopped to grab a Distance Band from a production-line belt rolling along beside him. He held up the platinum band to better admire it. The central strip of LEDs was inactive but it would flash red if the user stepped within two meters of an unregistered member outside the family bubble.

You'd be proud of what I've achieved, darling, Geist thought sadly. *If only you could see me now.*

Geist was of Austrian ancestry. His great grandparents, who were born and raised in Salzburg, Austria, a city near the German border, immigrated to Winnipeg, Manitoba two years following World War Two, in search of a better life.

In C2–, when he was eighteen, Geist started working for Canada Post, delivering mail like his father and grandfather. During his first week on the job, he'd delivered an envelope to a small house with a red door in the suburbs. As he'd hopped up the porch and opened the mailbox, the red door had opened, revealing a cute, freckled brunette in a red polka dot dress and pinned up hair. She was about the same age as him.

"Good morning," he said and tipped his cap.

The girl leaned against the doorframe, studying him. Strangers often gawked at him, for his pale skin, white hair, and crimson eyes. He learned to ignore the stares, but this young woman had destroyed his defenses, flooding him with old insecurities. He turned away and trotted back to his van.

He was halfway down the driveway when she called, "What's your name?"

He stopped and turned. "Walter. Walter Geist."

She smiled but stayed leaning against the doorframe. She crossed one ankle in front of the other. "I'm Ophelia. Ophelia Schmidt. I wondered who'd replace Gus. He was our old mailman."

"He's retired to Florida," Geist said and looked at his feet. He generally shied from people, having been an outcast his whole life, but women—especially pretty, young women— made him uncomfortable. "Well," he said without looking up, "it was a pleasure, ah, meeting you. I must be off now."

"Do you want to go on a date with me?"

His face suddenly started burning and he looked behind involuntarily. There was no one else around, so she'd evidently been talking to him. He poked a finger to his chest. "Who? Me?"

She giggled. "Yes, you. I find you . . . intriguing."

So, he took her to the local drive-in theater in his work van that Friday night, which played an old 1980 film titled *Brave New World.* They cuddled next to one another as they sat hypnotized watching the screen. Walter put an arm around her shoulder and she smiled. He fell in love with Ophelia Schmidt that very night, marrying her in the later half of C2–.

When COVID-19 arrived in Canada, claustrophobia set in every time Geist donned his mask; his legs trembled every step of his delivery route. He worried about catching COVID-19 and worried even more about Ophelia, five months pregnant with their first baby.

Six months into the pandemic, as Spring was coaxing blooms from the trees, his delivery route took him past a group of about fifty protesters in the park, all huddled together like penguins in a snowstorm. Walter's interest got the better of him and he crossed the street to find out what was going on. Many of the protesters held homemade signs aloft bearings slogans: *Oxygen is Essential; My Body, My Choice; No More Masks.*

Geist gasped as he realized not a single individual followed public health orders to wear a mask or maintain any kind of social distancing.

The leader of the rally, a middle-aged, red-haired woman climbed onto the plinth of a bronze Sir John A. Macdonald statue. She lifted a megaphone to her mouth.

"Friends," she said, "thank you for coming out and showing the government that we will not be controlled." There was a smattering of applause and cheers from the group. The megaphone squealed a momentary burst of static and feedback. "It's time for the sheeple to wake up. This *plan*-demic will not dictate our lives. They want to vaccinate us so we can be microchipped. Like dogs and cats! What do we have to say about that?"

The woman held out her ear as the group chanted, "No way! No way! No way!"

Their leader beamed. "We'll show them what they're dealing with. We're going to march on parliament and demand the lawmakers to give us back our freedom!"

The small crowd shouted its agreement and the red-haired woman jumped off the statue and led the group through the park. Walter stood frozen with his back against an oak tree, trying to conceal himself from the approaching crowd, but they didn't seem to notice him as they passed. Once the park emptied, he sighed and headed back to work.

Four days later, Ophelia rolled over in bed and began to cough. Geist immediately sprang out of bed, holding a cotton sheet for shield protection.

"Darling, you're sick," he said.

She coughed a little more. "I'm fine, it's just a tickle in my throat. It's not COVID." She smiled faintly. "I haven't been around anyone for the past six months."

But I have, he thought with guilt, and in his mind, he saw the unmasked protesters in their close huddle. He shook his head. What were the odds of him catching anything from such a gathering? He hadn't been too close to them. *I don't even have any symptoms. I couldn't have brought it home.*

The next day, Ophelia developed a fever and chills. "That's it," Geist told her. "I'm taking you to the hospital. Let me grab your coat."

"No, Walt," she cried from the bed. "I don't want to go. What if it's not COVID, and I show up to the ER and get it there? You've heard the stories. The hospitals are jammed with COVID-19 patients."

"Think about the baby, darling. Let's go, just to be safe."

He held out his hand and she reluctantly took it. He helped her to the car, double-masking himself and trying not to breathe too deeply around her.

At the hospital, he parked in the expecting mothers' parking spot. As he was helping her manoeuvre herself out of the passenger door, she cried out in agony, clutching her belly.

"What is it?" he said. "What's happened?"

"It's the baby," she gasped and fell to her knees beside the car. There was a sudden bloom of blood on the front of her dress.

"Help!" Geist shouted. "Someone! I need help!"

Two masked security guards ran through the sliding ER doors and across the parking lot. They pulled Ophelia to her feet and took her weight between them, her arms around their shoulders. They hustled into the hospital and Geist struggled to keep up with them. They put her in a wheelchair and wheeled her into a quiet room.

An ER nurse appeared just a few moments later and swabbed Ophelia's nose, and did the same for Geist before she left. Ophelia moaned on the bed as the ER doctor came in, dressed in what looked like a spacesuit. Geist took a step forward.

"I'm sorry, sir," the doctor said, politely but firmly. "Only patients and staff can be in here. No family members, I'm afraid." She put a gloved palm on his chest, her attention distracted by her pager. When she looked up at Geist, her eyes showed the usual shock at his appearance; even doctors weren't immune to it. Geist ignored it.

"We're expecting a baby," he said. "I need to be with my wife!"

"I understand, but there's nothing I can do. It's hospital protocol. Feel free to video chat with her at any time. In the meantime, we'll do our best to keep you updated."

The doctor ushered him through the door and out into the corridor, where one of the security guards smiled sympathetically and led him out of the hospital.

Behind him, as the sliding doors shut him out, he heard Ophelia cry out.

*

Walter paced the house for the next two days, skipping meals and skipping work. There had been no word from the hospital about his wife's status, but when his phone finally rang, he sprang onto it.

"Yes, hello, its Walter Geist."

"Mister Geist, this is Juliette, the ER physician. I met you the other day."

Walter did away with the formalities.

"How's Ophelia?"

"I'm very sorry, Walter, but I have some bad news. She lost the baby."

Geist's knees suddenly unhinged, and he stumbled backwards. He would have fallen to the floor if a chair hadn't struck the back of his legs, causing him to fall onto that instead. "That can't be right." he said and clasped his forehead. "Please, no." He burst into tears.

"Walter," the doctor said gently, "these are unprecedented times. This is not the way I'd want to break this to you. Your wife's swab came back positive for COVID-19. She deteriorated very quickly after arrival, I'm afraid. We had to move her to the ICU. She's intubated."

ICU? Intubated? What was this mad woman talking about?

"Walter, are you there?"

"Yes."

"She's going to be staying with us for a while. We'll update you along the way, okay?"

"Yes. Sure."

"Also, your swab had returned positive for COVID-19 as well. Have you been feeling ill at all? Do you know where you could've caught it? We need this information for contact tracing purposes."

He hung up the phone.

*

Two months later, Geist pulled up to the hospital doors. Ophelia was finally being discharged from Intensive Care Unit.

He jumped from the car and ran to the doors where a nurse in a yellow gown was rolling a wheelchair down the access ramp.

"Darling!" he cried. "At last! How are you?" To the nurse, he said, "I'll take it from here, thanks."

Ophelia slowly looked up at him. Her brunette hair had thinned dramatically. Her frame was frail, at least thirty pounds lighter. Geist had been told about her condition before picking her up, but her emaciated state was still a shock. Nasal prongs attached to her nostrils. She required continuous supplemental oxygen to breathe, and while her infectious symptoms had resolved, she had ongoing breathing difficulties. She gazed up at him with dead eyes.

He gave a weak smile and helped her into the car.

The next few months proved difficult. Geist had to quit work to look after Ophelia full-time. He helped her with bathing, dressing, and moving around. She hardly ate anything and barely spoke. He carried a guilt as heavy as an anchor, but he never admitted he caused the avalanche onto their lives. What good would that knowledge do her anyway?

Four months later, they were watching the evening news from the living room couch, eating microwaved fried chicken and mashed potatoes. The TV showed a blonde news anchor, reporting yet again on the COVID-19 situation.

"The public continues to defy the advice of health officials," the reporter said gravely and shook her perfectly coiffured hair away from her face. "This has caused a record-breaking count of positive COVID-19 cases in Canada. As we near the pandemic's one-year anniversary, doctors continue to raise the alarm, warning it is far past the point to flatten the curve. A second wave is inevitable."

"Something needs to change!" Geist shouted in sudden frustration and slammed his fist against the coffee table.

Ophelia wheezed next to him, and Geist made a conscious effort to calm himself. "What do you think, darling?" he said, to try and spark some kind of conversation that wasn't about her ongoing disability.

Ophelia stared at him vacantly, mumbling.

"What did you say?"

"Kill me."

"Kill you?" Not this again. He'd heard her say it so many times now. "How could you say such a thing?"

"Kill me," she wheezed. "Kill me. Kill me. *Kill me!*"

Geist stood up and backed away to the kitchen. He stood next to the microwave with tears streaming down his face. From the living room, he heard Ophelia sobbing in the darkness.

That night, he lay awake in bed, facing the window. Ophelia snored in deep rattling gasps. Geist peered at her in the dark, at the oxygen tank next to her bedside table, feeding her nasal prongs with a mist of oxygen.

My poor Ophelia, he thought. *This is all my fault. If only I'd stuck to my route.*

He laid there for hours, contemplating his life, and Ophelia's. The decision was clear—he needed to do what the politicians wouldn't do. He needed to find a way of enforcing behavioral changes on a global scale, one that governments would agree on if it was pitched in the right way.

The public had their chance to comply. Now we need to do it my way.

He sat up suddenly and grabbed his pillow. He turned to Ophelia. Her brow was furrowed, her sallow face pinched and bony. Her rattling breath was labored.

"Hush now, my darling," he whispered. "It'll soon be over."

He pressed his pillow gently over her face and bore down on it with all his weight. For a moment there was perfect silence and stillness. Then Ophelia began to thrash and buck against him. Beneath the pillow, her screams were weak and muffled.

"No more suffering," Geist said. "I'm here with you."

She thrashed frantically for less than a minute. And then she went limp.

*

The roar of clattering machinery drew Geist out of his memory and back into the real world. He felt the brand new, unprogrammed Distance Band in his fist and stared at it for a long moment before throwing it back onto the production-line belt. He turned away and strode on through the factory, smoothing the fine, soft leather of his coat with both hands.

"The world is a better place now," he said quietly, under his breath. "All thanks to you, my darling."

Chapter Thirteen

Noah was six years old. He was running around the empty park on a warm summer day, laughing as sand squished underneath the feet of his white HAZMAT suit. He kept trying to steal the attention of his mom, Olivia, who was sitting quietly on a bench in her own HAZMAT suit. She had a twinkle in her eyes and she waved at Noah each time he passed her by.

A squirrely boy around Noah's age showed up with his own mom. Mother and son both had bleached white hair and wore tattered clothes without HAZMAT suits, which Noah found peculiar. The only protection they had from the outside world was the red cotton masks covering their noses and mouths. The boy's mom sat next to Olivia, who slid away along the bench and flashed the woman a nasty look. Noah didn't quite understand why she made that face, though she always commented on people who only wore a mask against COVID-37. She worried they posed a safety risk for others.

Noah turned his attention to the climbing frame in front of him and climbed it to the top, where there was a landing of sorts. He looked over at his mom who seemed more tense than ever.

"Mom!" he called. "Watch me go down the slide!"

She finally glanced up at him, waving again. Noah grabbed the handles and launched himself down the swirly yellow slide, landing in the sand directly facing his mom.

The squirrely boy saw how much fun Noah was having and said, "Hey! Can I play with you?"

"Yeah, sure," Noah said but he glimpsed his mom's frown behind her face-shield.

The white-haired boy jumped next to Noah and their Distance Bands started flashing red and beeping. Noah's parents had trained him well. He backed away from the other boy, trying to re-establish a six-foot gap, but as he did, the white-haired boy followed him, getting closer. Their Distance Bands beeped more noisily.

"You back away from my son right now!" Olivia shouted, pointing at the white-haired boy.

He put his hands up, as if she'd pointed a gun at him, and stopped in his tracks. "I'm sorry. I just wanted to play with my new friend," the boy said, voice trembling.

"You want to play with others, you stay six feet apart," Olivia snapped. "You got that?" As she sat back down, the boy's mom glared at her.

"Don't you dare speak to my son like that," the woman said and stood up. "Apologize to him, right now."

Noah didn't like arguments, so he sprinted across the sand and around the playground. The white-haired boy followed him, laughing, and they chased each other among the apparatus, safely distanced. As they ran, the sky clouded over. The boy scaled the climbing frame until he reached the top landing. Noah was close behind when his new friend stared back at him and said, "See you at the bottom!"

Noah could still hear the two women arguing. As he grabbed the handles to catapult himself down the yellow slide, he heard a loud bang below. He launched himself down the slide and heard another bang. As he reached the bottom, he jumped into the sand and stood stock-still. His mouth fell open, but no sound came out.

The white-haired woman and her son were sprawled in the sand, face down. They were completely still, and the sand was soaked in blood, slowly turning black. Noah looked up for his mom, but she was gone. Snow started to drift from the low-hanging clouds and wind stirred the trees.

Instead of his mom, Noah saw a figure in a black HAZMAT suit. It marched toward him, and he noticed that the tinted face-shield was cracked down its center. The figure stopped, six feet in front of him. It removed its broken helmet. A woman with jet-black hair, olive skin, and blood-shot, hazel eyes glared at him.

She raised her gun, pointed it directly at his forehead, and fired.

Chapter Fourteen

Noah woke up screaming. He was slick with cold sweat. He sat up
and found himself in a makeshift hospital bed with his indoor garments
soaked; there was no sign of his HAZMAT suit. Bright lights all around
the room blinded him. His heart was pounding hard enough to leap from
his chest and his body was sore all over.

Where am I?

His mind was empty, and he couldn't remember what had led him
to this bed. Then it all came rushing back at once and he was so overcome
with nausea he had to lean over the side of the bed's railing to vomit.

"Easy, son," Eamon said. He was sitting in a chair to the left of the
bed, still wearing his HAZMAT suit. Noah realized he was inside a glass
box of a room, like a lab rat. Various medical personnel sat at desks
beyond the glass walls, taking notes and monitoring computers. Noah saw

he had cannulas in both arms, attached to IV lines. Bags of solution and medication hung on poles above, and his vitals were shown on the mirror in front of him.

"You're okay, Noah," Eamon said. "These are some of those colleagues I was telling you about. We made it to Calgary safe and sound."

"What is this place? What happened to me?"

"We're in one of four patient observation units. At the medical bay inside an airplane hangar."

"Hold up—airplane hangar?" Noah had never even seen an airplane, let alone contemplated hiding in an airplane hangar.

"The authorities aren't interested in ancient ruins like this," Eamon said. "It's been abandoned for decades. We're safe here."

Nausea swept over Noah again, but this time he didn't vomit. "I feel awful," he said. "Like I've been run over by a train." His stomach rolled and gurgled, and he closed his eyes to focus on not vomiting.

"You're in withdrawal," Eamon said. "From your antidepressant. Your body had gotten accustomed to Lumox after so many years. But you've been without it for three days now. That's why you feel so . . . rough. It'll pass soon enough, trust me."

"I've been out for three days?" Noah gasped. That meant today was Monday, November 25, C49+. "I don't even remember getting here. Where's my medication?" he said, shifting in his bed.

"Relax, son," Eamon said and placed a calm hand on Noah's chest. "It's best you're off that stuff."

"No. I need my medication."

"Ask yourself this—have you ever felt depressed?"

Noah thought about it. "No. I've never felt much of anything, if I really think about it."

"Exactly," Eamon said. "I've been off my antidepressant for three years now, and I've never felt better in my life. We've been brainwashed by the government and the media into taking this pill, to feel nothing."

"You can't blame society for choosing to be happy," Noah snapped. "We weren't exactly living exciting lives. The pandemic made sure of that."

Eamon smiled sadly. "You sound just like your Grandpa John. I think he prepped all year for your birthday lectures . . . much to my displeasure. Do you remember your fifteenth birthday?"

"Of course," Noah said. Grandpa John had spoken of his younger years, when he had been a practicing family doctor. Noah could remember what he'd said almost word for word.

"Those early COVID years were tough," Grandpa John had told him. "On top of a raging pandemic, mental health became an additional crisis. You're too young to know any different, but mandatory self-isolation took its toll on people. At first, most were hopeful and found clever ways to stay connected with friends and family. I remember scrolling through social media and seeing viral trends taking hold. 'Take a shot, send a shot' was a popular one. The active ones participated in 'do 10 push-ups, send 10 push-ups.' But the good times soon faded.

"By 2022, many people had fallen into depression, whether there was a history of mood disorders or not. The human psyche could only resist such hardship for so long before it cracked. We were used to freedom and we dreamed of a return to pre-COVID times. Overnight, we became prisoners in our own homes. Eventually, a new online trend went viral—'see a suicide, do a suicide.' We lost so many people as a side effect of the pandemic."

"That's why we take our Lumox, isn't it?" Noah had asked.

"Yes, it is. It's a bit ironic that self-isolation orders for public safety generated so many drug overdoses, as well as domestic violence, racial hate crimes, and mental health disorders. In the end, bylaws were introduced, compelling everyone to take a daily antidepressant. To keep us happy. Or, as I would rather call it, to keep us numb."

Noah remembered that conversation so clearly, and now, the loss of his grandparents suddenly flooded back into his memory so forcefully, that for a second, he couldn't breathe. He gasped and tears sprang into his eyes.

"How'd I end up in here?" Noah asked when he was able to speak.

"Once we made it to Calgary, I had to get you under medical observation while we weaned you off the Lumox." Eamon said.

"Dad, what the hell happened back on the highway? Last thing I remember is seeing Jasmine before I blacked out. Why was she attacking us? What the hell is going on?"

Eamon sighed. Noah watched his father, hunched over with his elbows on his knees and his head hanging. Eventually, he said, "After your mother died, I realized the system is broken. Not just in healthcare, but the whole of society. If it weren't for fear of COVID-37, your mom might have sought medical attention earlier . . . and still been here. After her passing, I vowed to do what I could to fix the system. But I soon came to understand that everything seemed to be connected to OWN Industries—or rather the One World Network. So, instead of trying to find a way to fix the system, I looked for a way to break it."

"I don't see what this has to do with Jas—"

Eamon waved a dismissive hand. "These past few years, I've done everything I can to learn about OWN's operations and intelligence. I made connections with people fighting the same fight, exploring ways to take down OWN. I thought I was being careful, inconspicuous. I had no idea there were always eyes on me. Jasmine didn't come into our lives by chance, son. She was strategically placed there, by OWN Industries."

Noah gaped at him. This was crazy, like one of those illegal conspiracy theories that sometimes popped up briefly online about the origins of COVID, or why no vaccines worked against the various mutations that had sprung up over the years.

"She took a position at my clinic so she could gather intel for Walter Geist," Eamon went on. "Simple as that. She was charming, no doubt about it, and like the fool they took me for, I fell in love with her." Eamon covered his face-shield with his hands.

"She was a *spy*?"

Eamon nodded. "But not just an ordinary spy. She's an OWN-operated and trained assassin."

Noah felt like his brain might explode, or at least short-circuit from over-computing. "But why did she choose you?"

Eamon looked up at his son and raised an eyebrow. He smiled a tiny smile.

"That came out wrong," Noah said sheepishly. "I mean, what makes you so special?"

Eamon was laughing now.

"Let me try that again. What reasons did she have to spy on you?"

Eamon shrugged. "OWN Industries holds shares in so much of the world's post-COVID market. I appeared on their radar with an innovative idea they hadn't come up with themselves. It was bound to raise some eyebrows. OWN has close ties with government; their agents are everywhere, keeping tabs on anyone with the potential to disrupt the status quo. There aren't many original thoughts or concepts these days, thanks to media indoctrination. Unfortunately, I was so focused on dismantling OWN, it just never occurred to me that my inner bubble could betray me.

It had only been the past few days I'd felt something off about Jasmine. Call it a gut feeling."

Outside the room, someone started banging on the glass wall. A tall white man with short grey and white hair stood there in a navy-blue HAZMAT suit. It bore decorative war medals on its left breast. His eyes were stone-black and his craggy face was carved with deep lines. Noah guessed he was in his eighties.

Eamon immediately stood up and saluted the figure. "General Vizor," he said. "I was wondering when you'd be back at home base. It's a pleasure to see you."

"I wish I could say the same, *Doctor* Teslow," General Vizor snarled back. He had a deep, raspy voice. "Please exit the patient observation unit immediately. I need to have a word with you."

Eamon squeezed Noah's arm and made his way to the Disinfectant Chamber at the far end of the room. It was another minute before Noah saw his father exit and move toward the General on the other side of the glass.

Without warning, Vizor grabbed Eamon by the chest of his suit and flung him against the glass wall. The thud was loud enough that Noah jumped and many of the people in the monitoring room stopped what they were doing to watch.

"How could you be so *stupid*?" Vizor roared. "You brought your son into my operation? *Really*? You've jeopardized everything we've worked so hard for." He slammed Eamon against the wall again and if he hadn't been tethered to his IV drips, Noah would have rushed out to help.

"I didn't have a choice," Eamon gasped. "I tried to keep my family out of it, but things got complicated. He was in grave danger, General. I couldn't leave him at the mercy of the police. I couldn't lose him . . . not after losing Olivia."

Slowly, Vizor lowered Eamon back onto his feet. "You make me sick," he muttered and turned away. "Clean up your mess. I've come too far to have your boy lead the authorities here. Or worse, get us all killed." He stalked off.

"He's a good kid," Eamon shouted after him. "We'll find a way for him to be useful. You can trust him!"

Vizor stopped and looked over his shoulder. "How can you say that when you were so easily deceived by your *wife*?" He shook his head and walked away.

Eamon raised his hand, and even from within the glass room, he could see his dad's body trembling. He took a step forward and cried, "Because he's your grandson!"

Chapter Fifteen

Noah remained in the patient observation unit for the next week. His father visited him for a few hours every day, to check up on him. Today, he stood next to Noah's bed and regarded him closely.

"How you feeling, son?"

Noah sat up. "Like I'm awake for the first time in my life. You were right about the medication." Without the drug in his system, he felt sharper than he could have imagined; colors shone more vividly, sounds were clearer, textures were intensely real to his touch. Even the smell and taste of familiar foods were new and exciting.

"Dad, why didn't you tell me about General Vizor before?" he said. The maternal side of his family had always been unknown to him, though not because of a lack of curiosity.

Eamon gave him a half-smile. "You mean your other grandpa?"

"I guess." Noah couldn't fathom having any relation with the gruff old man.

"We thought we were doing you a service, your mother and I. We thought it was best to leave certain things in the past."

"Dad, you've sheltered me all my life. And look where we are now." He gripped the rail of his bed until his knuckles turned white. "I need you to tell me about my family. Now."

Eamon sighed and sat on the chair next to the IV pole and monitors. "You're right," he said. "You deserve to know. Where would you like me to start?"

Noah held his father's gaze. "The beginning's usually the best place."

Eamon smiled ruefully. "Sure. Well, your mom was raised in a military family. Her father, Bernard Vizor, was born and raised in Ottawa. When he was sixteen, his parents allowed him to join the army. One year into his service, he was transferred to Saskatoon, where he met his future wife, your other grandmother, Thea. She was a waitress at Bernard's favorite restaurant."

Eamon smoothed his suit's pants and looked up at the IV bag hanging above him. Noah realized it was hard for his father to tell this story, but he needed to know, however his father felt. "Go on," he said.

Eamon nodded. "They fell madly in love," he said, "and spent every waking moment together, when he wasn't training, of course. In C18–, when he was only eighteen years old, Bernard was deployed to

Afghanistan, along with many other young men and women. The fight then wasn't against COVID, but against terrorism. Bernard and Thea decided to postpone their marriage, but he promised that when—or if—he returned, they would get married.

"He spent five long years in Afghanistan, with only occasional brief returns home. The war brought out the worst in many people, but Bernard demonstrated unrivaled courage, resilience, and leadership. He was promoted rapidly through the ranks, and by the time he returned to Canada in C13–, he was a Major."

Noah had seen a few old-time movies about war, all of which fascinated him. The idea of troops being used as pawns, in some unimaginably complex chess game, claiming one territory over the next, was unfathomable to him. In C49+, all you needed was the threat of long-range missiles to keep the peace.

"Keep going," Noah said.

"Back in Saskatoon, the first thing Bernard did was purchase a ring. He proposed to Thea the same day and they got married the following year. Given his rank and ongoing potential, he was rotated back to Ottawa and Thea moved with him. They settled down in the quiet suburbs.

"From what your mom told me, all was fine at first, but Bernard found himself so preoccupied with work that he neglected his wife completely. He justified everything with the excuse that he was serving and protecting his country. By C1–, he was made General, but at the same time, Thea gave him an ultimatum: it was either work or marriage. Bernard never gave her a straight answer, and they eventually decided that a child might save their marriage.

"In the wake of COVID-19 and heading into C1+, Bernard became even more obsessed with work. That same year, Thea became pregnant. She admitted to her husband that she'd been battling her own war for years—she'd effectively been isolated well before COVID-19 and succumbed to major depression. With talks of border closures on the horizon, Thea made the difficult decision to leave her husband. She secretly booked a one-way ticket to Saskatoon to be with her family. She knew her husband would be outraged, but she needed to be selfish for her own physical and mental health during a pandemic. Your mom was born in C2+, supported and loved by Thea and her family. Border closures meant Bernard never got a chance to become the father he wanted to be."

"He never met Mom?" Noah asked.

"Never, but he tried. As your mom grew older, of course she asked about her absent father. Thea deflected the questions for years, but eventually she caved in and told your mother about him—and how to reach him. They exchanged emails despite him being wanted by the government, and that was as much of a relationship as they had. Even on our wedding day, General Vizor couldn't be there."

"He never reached out to you? Even after Mom died?"

Eamon frowned. "He blamed me for her death."

"It wasn't your fault. The medical system failed her. We know that. How could he blame you?"

Outside the glass room, Noah glimpsed Vizor as he appeared in the monitoring room for his daily rounds, slithering through the desks like a snake in the grass. He stopped outside Noah's observation unit and glared in.

Eamon looked up and stared back at him. "He blamed me," he said, "because he couldn't fathom how a physician didn't pick up on his own wife's diagnosis."

Chapter Sixteen

Noah donned his HAZMAT suit inside the Disinfectant Chamber of the observation unit while Eamon waited outside for him. Noah was scheduled for a tour of the abandoned hangar. He exited the Disinfectant Chamber and joined his dad in the room full of monitoring equipment. Nobody paid him any attention.

"Ready?" Eamon said.

"Sure," Noah replied. "Let's see what we got here."

They crossed the room and Eamon led him through a fire door into a huge space beyond. As he stepped out into it, the first thing he noticed was the enormous, curved roof, arching far above his head.

"Pretty neat, huh?" Eamon said. "It's a one-way glass ceiling. We benefit from natural light from inside, but nobody can see in from outside. We're able to work freely."

Noah whistled through his lips. "It must've cost a fortune."

Eamon smiled. "I didn't have to pay for it. Now, the dormitories are in the south-east corner of the hangar. You'll be sharing a bunker with me."

Noah nodded and looked around the huge interior space of the hangar. It was divided into obvious sections, with groups of people working around large rectangular wooden tables. Each table bore computers, banks of TV monitors, radio receivers, miscellaneous office supplies, and old-fashioned devices bristling with knobs, dials, and antennae. This underground network didn't seem to have access to the latest tech. In the distance, Noah saw General Vizor striding around in his navy-blue HAZMAT suit, hands clasped behind his back, monitoring the work in progress at various tables. He noticed armed guards in camo-green HAZMAT suits stationed along various points in the hangar.

"This is quite the operation," he said. Noah edged closer to Eamon as they passed one of the guards.

"Don't worry, they're here to protect us," Eamon said. "From any outside interference."

"So, who—or what—are we working for?" Noah asked.

Eamon laughed. "General Vizor, your grandfather, calls it the First Legion of Insurrection against Government Heralds and Tyrants. Bit of a mouthful, isn't it? But he's the head of operations, so that's what it's called. The rest of us call it the FLIGHT network. He founded it in C10+. Its whole purpose was to strip power from totalitarian governments and their little brother, OWN."

As they moved through the hangar, Eamon nodded to various people at their workstations. They wore a variety of colored HAZMAT suits, and they all politely nodded back at him, but they seemed too preoccupied with their work to converse.

"What are they working on?" Noah finally asked as they made their way toward the west wall of the hangar.

"Everybody here has their own skillsets and they're using them to help FLIGHT in its war against OWN Industries and the government. There's a six-member working group at each table. You'll learn more from the team you've been assigned to. Our team."

"*Our* team? Dad, I don't know how useful I can be here. I don't have any valuable skills or experience for this operation."

"Don't be so naïve, son," Eamon said. "Everyone has a role to play, whether they know it or not. You'll find yours when the time's right."

Noah was just a first-year university student who'd spent his whole life in isolation. What could he possibly add to these experts that Vizor had assembled? He was out of his league.

They arrived at their workstation, where five people were huddled around a TV on the table, their face-shields reflecting the screen.

"Hey, team," Eamon said. "I'd like to introduce you all to my son—"

"Shh," a dark-haired young woman said, putting a finger to her face-shield in front of her lips. "Can't you see we're trying to watch something important here?"

Next to her, a middle-aged black man said, "We're just getting to the good part, doc. Come take a look."

Eamon and Noah walked around the table and stood behind the group. They were watching a news channel, where the same blonde news anchor Noah had watched at home was reporting the evening news. He recognized her prominent cheekbones and pearly, translucent eyes.

"Police authorities have still not identified the whereabouts of two fugitives from Saskatoon, Saskatchewan," she said. "The respected doctor and innovator, and his son, were last seen leaving Villa Salud care facility on November twenty-second, around eight in the evening."

A picture popped up next to the anchor's head showing Eamon and Noah, crystal clear for the world to see. It was a photo Jasmine had taken last summer, as they'd all relaxed on the deck.

"Oh, no," Noah groaned.

Without turning, the young woman held up a hand and hissed, *"Shh!"*

"Drone footage reveals both Eamon and Noah Teslow fleeing from police after curfew," the anchor continued. The screen cut to a video clip from a drone camera as it chased them through the atrium of Villa Salud. "Honored End-Generationers and family members John and Noelle Teslow were found dead in their long-term care pod and while authorities are refusing to jump to conclusions, police sources have confirmed that both fugitives have deactivated their Distance Bands. These same sources have confirmed that police are investigating a possible defection to an underground terrorist organization, and potential attendance to Super-Spreader events to become Hackers."

"Nobody's going to believe that," Noah said and looked at the group, then at his father. "Are they?"

Nobody answered, but the news anchor said, "At this time, police have detained Justus Okenawah, manager of Villa Salud, for further questioning. The authorities have asked the public to remain vigilant and to report any suspicious activity immediately. We'll keep you updated on this story as it develops. Stay tuned and stay safe."

The young woman turned off the TV and spun around in her chair to face Noah. She extended her right hand and said, "Well then, it is *so* nice to finally meet you."

Noah extended his own hand and she gripped it firmly.

"Welcome to FLIGHT!" she said, smiling fiercely.

Chapter Seventeen

The FLIGHT team welcomed Noah warmly. Teams usually consisted of six members, but an exception had been made for him and he sat at the rectangular table amongst his new colleagues. Although they all wore HAZMAT suits, Noah couldn't help feeling uncomfortable in such close proximity to the others. He'd been conditioned by his Distance Band to stay six feet away from anyone beyond his immediate household and he felt weirdly vulnerable—naked even—without it now.

The dark-haired young woman sat to Noah's left. She was about his age, with long hair, almond-colored eyes, and a cute little nose. When she smiled, her teeth were perfectly white, which contrasted sharply with her blossom-red HAZMAT suit.

"I'm Cecilia Flores," she said in a voice as smooth as honey.

"I'm Noah Teslow," he said, though for a moment, he hadn't been sure he'd be able to speak at all.

A fair-skinned redhead in her early sixties said, "We know who you are, kiddo." She sat on Cecilia's left, in a HAZMAT suit with a yellow-black honeycomb pattern. "Everyone in this place does. How you feelin' without that junk in your system?" Cecilia nudged her with her elbow, and she blinked at Noah. "Oh right, intros," she said. "I'm Nikita. Nikita Vansberg. You can call me Nik."

Noah gave her an awkward half-wave. "Nice to meet you."

Eamon sat on Noah's right. "Why don't I finish the rest of the intros?" he said. "Then we can get back to business." The team nodded. "Across the table, we have Goddfrey Williams," Eamon said. "Former media mogul with thirty years' experience in the entertainment business."

Goddfrey was a black gentleman in his late sixties, with short, springy grey and black hair. He wore a light brown HAZMAT suit. "Pleasure to meet you, Noah," he said. His voice was deep and resonant, perfect for a guy in the media spotlight. "Most people around here know me by my TV moniker, Goodwill. I'm sure we'll get along just fine." He had soft facial features that were sharpened by his dark, translucent eyes and when he winked at Noah, he smiled a smile that had probably sealed hundreds of million-dollar media deals.

"Over here, we have Viktor Ivanov," Eamon said. "A former nuclear physicist for the United States government, now a full-time lab researcher. We're very fortunate to have him on our program." He bowed to the most senior member of the group.

Viktor sat opposite Noah with both hands clasped on the table, wearing a light grey HAZMAT suit that matched his hair and bushy eyebrows. He closed his eyes and gave the slightest of nods to Noah.

"And finally," Eamon said, "we have one of our newest recruits, Tommy Chin." Tommy wore a forest green HAZMAT suit and sat at the far right side of the table. "He was studying at UBC in Vancouver, working toward a computer science major. He *was*, until he hacked into the Canadian government's computer system and stole masses of information. Many of those documents are still encrypted, but we're working on breaking the codes. It's all extra ammo for our fight."

Tommy was of Asian heritage but to Noah, he looked smug and self-satisfied, like he knew something the rest of the group didn't.

"Why would you do something like that?" Noah said. "I mean, you weren't even recruited by FLIGHT at that point."

"Why did you leave your house so close to curfew?" Tommy fired back. "I did it for the hell of it."

"So, you're a hacker."

"I don't like to use the term . . . Hacker. Most people interpret it a little differently these days, don't you think?" Tommy grinned but gave Noah a sly look. "I prefer techno-pirate."

Noah was so close to rolling his eyes at this computer nerd's self-importance that he almost had to close them completely. "Techno-pirate? Wow."

"General Vizor sought me out before the authorities could," Tommy said, either ignoring or missing Noah's sarcasm. "He recognized my potential, which is more than I can say for yourself. You're only here because of special family privileges."

The rest of the team looked at Noah, as if waiting for a rebuttal. But he had nothing to say. He'd been thinking the same himself. Though he didn't need a jerk like Tommy Chin pointing it out to everybody.

"That's enough," Eamon said firmly. "We'll be spending a lot of time together, so put aside any quarrels you may have. As I said, we need to get back to business."

"Oops," Tommy said and snickered.

With introductions over, everyone got back to work, on computers, tablets, or old-fashioned paper.

Noah leaned over, as close to Eamon as he could get. "Um, dad," he whispered. "I think now might be a good time to tell me exactly what it is we're working on."

Eamon raised his eyebrows. "Oh, I still haven't mentioned that yet?" he said with mock astonishment. "We're developing a COVID-37 vaccine."

Chapter Eighteen

Noah stared at his dad. "A vaccine? A potential cure for all of this?"

The implications were staggering. A vaccine would completely transform the world—no more Distance Bands, no more self-isolation, no more curfews, no more border closures.

"This is huge!" he cried.

"It really is," Eamon said proudly.

"The government never really had a vaccine in development, did they?" Noah asked. He thought of all the times he'd listened to Prime Minister Talbot's empty words of hope.

"Well . . . yes and no."

"How do you mean?"

"There never was a government-funded vaccine being produced for the public," Eamon said. "However, a vaccine *does* exist somewhere out there. The government and OWN had no financial cap on developing one. Many of the world's top scientists are in the pockets of the powerful. The truth is, an effective vaccine for COVID-37 *was* found . . . decades ago."

"Decades ago? There's been a vaccine out there for *decades*? Why don't we know about it?"

"Hardly anybody knows about it, Noah. We've been manipulated by the government and the media our whole lives. Don't get me wrong, the risk of COVID-37 is real, we can see that in its 45% death rate, across all age groups. That's a fact. But the government, together with OWN, have withheld a cure this whole time. It's literally criminal. Only the elite have received the vaccine." Eamon's jaw was clenched so tightly Noah could see the muscles standing out in his cheeks.

"Let me get this straight," Noah said. He felt lightheaded. "The 'elite' have been enjoying their risk-free private lives while the rest of us have been living with the crippling fear of COVID-37?"

Eamon nodded, as if he didn't dare allow himself to speak. Eventually, he said, "We're working on getting this type of information out to the public. We'll blow the roof off this whole thing."

The rest of the group shot Noah and Eamon irritated glances, but Eamon continued talking. "You haven't put it all together yet, have you?" he said.

Noah was starting to feel irritated himself. "How could I, when all I get are your cryptic words and half-truths? How could I come up with my own conclusions to this madness?"

Eamon laughed. "Fair enough. Let me explain one more thing, then we really must get back to work."

"Anytime would be nice," Cecilia Flores said without looking up from her computer.

Eamon ignored her. "Remember how I told you I was visiting Grandpa John and Grandma Noelle more often?"

"Yes, I remember. Visiting them without me."

Eamon waved his hand impatiently. "Well, like I said, your grandparents' quality of life was poor. Their world was limited to a pod, and their health was deteriorating. They wanted more for this world. They wanted a world free from COVID-37."

"Dad, please. Get to the point."

"Okay, okay. Your grandparents asked for medical assistance in dying, but they kept insisting that they didn't want to die in vain. I discussed the FLIGHT network with them and they offered a brilliant solution: to take blood samples from them for analysis here at FLIGHT."

Noah felt like he was searching for a light switch in a dark room. "I guess that explains why they were hooked up to IVs," he said, though he could barely bring himself to think about those final moments, watching his grandparents sitting in their pod with the life drained out of them. "But why would FLIGHT need their blood?"

Cecilia grabbed a pen and gave Noah a look of utter annoyance. "Do you really need us to draw you a picture, Einstein?"

"Grandpa John and Grandma Noelle had COVID-37?" Noah spluttered.

"Bingo," Eamon said. "They knew their time was up so they volunteered to be injected with the COVID-37 virus. It's not easy to obtain a syringe of such hazardous material, but we have our means, and once administered, we let their bodies' immune systems do their magic. They knew they were unlikely to survive the infection."

"They surrendered their lives for science," Noah said. "For the chance that their bodies might develop some sort of immune response. For the chance that a vaccine could be developed from their sacrifice." A single tear spilled from his eye and rolled silently down his cheek.

"I hope you can understand that everything I—and they—did was for the greater good. They wanted a better future. For you, for me, and for the world."

"I understand, Dad. It must've been hard for you. But I get it now."

Eamon became suddenly bluff and hearty, though Noah had glimpsed the wetness in his dad's eyes too. "Right, well, that's enough of all that. I think the group would appreciate us joining them. Right?"

Cecilia looked up at him but said nothing. The rest ignored him.

"Right," Noah said, but he felt suddenly emboldened by FLIGHT's cause. A better world was waiting and he needed to be a catalyst for the change. "Let's get to work."

Chapter Nineteen

After a few days, the daily operations inside the dimly lit hangar became Noah's routine. Every morning at six, he and the other seven dozen FLIGHT recruits woke from their bunkers in the south-east corner of the building and headed to the cafeteria for breakfast. Packaged meals were provided once a week through a reliable—and secure—connection to the food industry. During breakfast, General Vizor, along with two of his advisors, Paul Colleaux and George Nibien, provided a debriefing: updates from each working group, recent government activity, potential recruits, and so on.

Following the debriefing, everyone worked at their stations until noon, when they broke for lunch. In the afternoon, members were encouraged to take shifts for simulation war training, which Noah discovered to be his favorite part of the day. The evening involved dinner at six followed by socializing, during which many members shared their personal stories. A lot of these stories involved the loss of loved ones who'd been abandoned and betrayed by the government when they needed support the most. The stories frequently ended with the FLIGHT member praising General Vizor for recruiting them and sewing purpose back into their lives.

"But how does he do it?" Noah asked Cecilia one night, when they were alone at a table. "How does he know who to recruit?"

"You mean how does he know who to trust?"

"Yes. There must be some wicked minds working against FLIGHT, posing as potential recruits." He thought of Jasmine and how flawlessly deceptive she had been.

Cecilia brushed off his concerns. "Relax, Noah. Your grandfather didn't get this far by luck. I don't think anyone here really understands his recruiting methods, but he knows what he's doing."

"Maybe," he said. "I'm not convinced, though. I mean, what about Tommy Chin?"

"What about him?"

"Well, he was picked up after hacking into the government's computer system and stealing a bunch of their documents."

"So?"

"So, who's to say he won't do the same to FLIGHT?"

Cecilia pondered the idea for a while. "Beats me," she said eventually. "I'm sure you could find the answer if you snuck into General Vizor's private office. Maybe he's hiding an anti-Distance Band tracker, or a teleportation tube, or a foolproof lie-detector." She laughed, and Noah smiled back at her.

Some members didn't care for the camaraderie of evening story-sharing and chose to work at their stations until lights-out at ten. Viktor Ivanov was one of them. He worked night and day in silence, often skipping meals to analyze data from the COVID-37 serum samples. He seemed determined to isolate the spike protein in the hopes of developing a vaccine. Many believed he'd joined FLIGHT to rewrite his legacy, just like General Vizor.

Earlier in the week, Noah had observed the brainy scientist polishing a medal, which he kept on the table next to his workspace.

"Hey, Viktor," Noah said. "What kind of medal is that?"

"Nobel Prize," Viktor said indifferently.

"Whoa." He leaned in to get a closer look at it. "What did you do to win *that*?"

Viktor continued polishing his medal with a clean handkerchief. Without looking up, he said, "Advancements in Quantum Chromodynamics." Though his accent was thick, Noah had no trouble understanding him.

"What?"

Goodwill leaned over, smiling toothily. "C'mon, Viktor. Give him a little more than that." He turned to Noah and fixed him with his dark, translucent eyes. "The man's a genius. Before COVID, he worked at CERN. With the use of the Large Hadron Collider, his research in subatomic particles gave us a better understanding of Quantum Chromodynamics, or QCD for short. Eventually, his work won him the Nobel Prize in Physics in C4–. Did I get it right, Viktor?"

"Something like that."

"Anyway," Goodwill continued, "he was in hot demand after that. The US military hired him and funded his work to develop unmatched nuclear weaponry to protect America from China and other hostile nations. He pushed the envelope and achieved yet again another major scientific breakthrough; he created the deadliest atomic bomb known to man."

Noah gawked at the old scientist, who remained unmoved by Goodwill's accolades. "Did they ever get used? The weapons?"

"No," Viktor said. "No one dare challenge US for their supreme weapons of mass destruction."

"But how did you end up at FLIGHT?"

Viktor put down his medal, as if annoyed by the distraction. "I chose wrong field of research. My bombs are big threat to world. I make pledge to self to save lives, not destroy them. Medal is reminder why I'm here. For General Vizor and vaccine research."

*

The daily schedule at FLIGHT was enforced to the minute by General Vizor. Noah had already violated the government-regulated curfew and he didn't intend breaking FLIGHT's protocol. Anyone doing so would land themselves in the Crypt, an underground area down the steps near the eastern wall of the hangar, next to General Vizor's office. The Crypt served as a brig or prison of sorts, one that the General constructed himself, though it had never been occupied, as no one was foolish enough to cross him. But it existed and Noah had no desire to become its first tenant.

Somehow, General Vizor scared Noah more than the government itself. Although his military history was well known, he remained an enigma; he didn't share personal stories and remained in his office most of the time, focused on his own business. During his rounds, he made no attempts to talk with Noah despite being—technically, at least—his grandfather. He didn't even make direct eye contact. In any case, as far as Noah was concerned, his only grandfather was John Teslow.

Despite being surrounded by strangers from all walks of life, after a couple weeks, Noah started to feel more at home. No one inside the hangar had an operating Distance Band or cellphone; every precaution was taken to eliminate the risk of exposing the operation.

Every afternoon, Noah and Cecilia headed to the Simulation Chamber, located at the north end of the hangar. The Simulation Chamber was their training ground, where they honed fighting skills against real-world threats, such as drones. Today, as they made their way toward the chamber, they were joined by Nikita, the retired police officer.

"Hey kiddos," she said. "Ready to get your butts whopped again?" She was hyped in her usual way. "Maybe this time you'll manage to kill half the drones I do. If you add your kills together."

"Very funny," Cecilia said and stuck out her tongue. "Enjoy your glory days while you can. Noah here is a natural. It's only a matter of time before he beats me *and* you."

Noah didn't like to boast but it was true; he was a born fighter. He had a natural athletic ability that he had never utilized until now. His reflexes were sharp and they'd become sharper since he'd stopped taking Lumox. Although he had only been in the chamber a handful of times, his drone-kills were increasing daily.

Nikita looked around. "Hm . . . looks like it's just us three again. I get why Viktor, Goodwill, and your father don't join us, but why not Tommy? Young 'uns are usually keen on shooting guns."

"He's probably a terrible aim," Noah said.

"Are we going to keep yapping or are we going to start shooting?" Cecilia said.

Nikita grinned and leaned over a chest with rows of palm-sized shiny metal orbs. She handed two to each of them. Noah grabbed a Hover helmet from one of the gym lockers next to the chest. The helmet emitted its characteristic white glow as he handed it to Cecilia.

"Aw, aren't you a gentleman," she said. "Don't get too soft now, Teslow. We got some training to do."

He laughed as he handed another helmet to Nikita, who said, "You guys head in, I'll be right behind you."

"Suit yourself," Noah said. He fitted the helmet over his face-shield.

Cecilia and Noah walked along a short corridor into a Disinfectant Chamber. Beyond that, they entered a high-ceilinged room similar in size as the hangar they came from, with reflective panels all over the walls. The room was filled with steel walls, stairways, and arched bridges, like an obstacle maze of sorts. Noah waved at some of the other recruits who finished their training session and exited the same way they came in.

Suddenly, the helmet's clear visor tracked the room's panels and rendered them as a wireframe model in front of Noah's eyes. A couple seconds later, the wireframe melted away and an urban landscape appeared, filling his field of vision. The ceiling was replaced with a dark, stormy sky. Lightning flashed in the distance and the helmet's speakers sounded with distant thunder.

Noah clicked a button on each of his orbs, which transformed into two weapons, designed by General Vizor himself: On his left arm, he now wore a transparent bubble shield with *FLIGHT* etched on it in large lettering. His right arm was enclosed within a phase-shift gun, which reminded Noah of old artillery cannons. The shield and gun were featherweight and he moved in fluid motions with them equipped. He gazed at the surrounding skyscrapers, and a swarm of drones descending toward them.

Nikita appeared behind Cecilia and stared up at the drones. She was equipped with her own bubble shield and gun. "Welcome to the virtual concrete jungle," she intoned and grinned.

They lifted their right arms in unison and charged their guns.

Chapter Twenty

Nightfall draped itself over the hangar; through the glass ceiling, the sky was studded with specks of stars. The half-crescent moon winked at Noah and Cecilia, who were both seated on an upturned empty crate at the back of the huddle of people.

Other FLIGHT members were seated on an assortment of crates, facing a holographic bonfire in the western corner of the hangar.

He glanced over at Cecilia. Her eyes danced with the flickering flames. "You ever think about what you'd do career-wise if you weren't working for FLIGHT?"

"Hm, I'd like to think an airline pilot. Travel the world and explore its wonders. You? Follow in your dad's footsteps in medicine?"

"I could never. Dad was a role model and community leader back home before we ran away. I'm neither of those things."

"You're being too hard on yourself. You've got the grit to be a physician too."

"Maybe." He cleared his throat and said, "I've got this nagging thought and I need to tell someone I trust before it drives me crazy."

She didn't look at him. "Yeah? What's that?"

"What happens to us if we never find a solution for COVID-37?"

She laughed sweetly. "Worst case scenario? You're stuck with me for eternity."

"Wouldn't be the worst thing," he said and felt his face growing hot, despite his suit's cooling mechanism. "But you've been here a lot longer than I have. How do you deal with the prospect of never getting out of here?"

Cecilia shrugged. "I remember what brought me here in the first place." She finally turned and faced him. "I want to play a game with you. Truth or dare."

"Really?"

"Really."

"Okay," he said. "Truth."

She nodded, as if she'd expected his response. "What is it you want most in this life, Noah Teslow?"

He contemplated the question for a few seconds. "Same thing as everyone, I guess. To find a cure for the pandemic."

She rolled her eyes. "Come on," she said and laughed again. "That's the best you can come up with?"

"What's wrong with that? Don't you want the same?"

"Of course, but it wouldn't be my first choice," she said evenly.

"Yeah?" Noah leaned back on the crate as if he were the coolest guy who ever lived. As long as she couldn't see his burning face. "What's your story anyway, CeCe? I've sat next to you for the last few weeks and I still don't know who you are." He leaned forward again. "Who's the woman behind the HAZMAT suit?" he said in his best *Batman* voice.

"You want to know about little old me?" she said and pressed a hand to her chest. "It isn't much of a story, I must warn you. Not a happy one, anyway."

"Try me."

"Well, my story begins on the west side of Saskatoon."

"We grew up in the same city and didn't even know it?"

"We sure did. I was eight years old at the time, living with my mom, dad, and fourteen-year-old brother Jose. We had what rich people call 'a modest house'. It's not what I would call it. My parents always struggled to make ends meet but I didn't know any better. I was just a little girl who loved shooting her brother with a Nerf gun."

"That explains so much already."

"My parents worked at the local grocery store as clerks. They couldn't afford HAZMAT suits, so they made do with simple bandanas over their faces for protection. This was a low-income neighborhood— very low—and people couldn't afford delivery services, so they shopped in person. They actually came to the store, with cash. Imagine that."

She looked at him pointedly and Noah swallowed hard. He wasn't responsible for the privilege he'd grown up with, but he had so little experience of how things were for other people. He shifted uncomfortably on the crate. "Yeah," he said awkwardly. "Imagine."

"It was ten years ago," Cecilia went on. "My mom and dad left for work that morning as usual. Jose was at home to look after me. And everything changed.

"They were always home by five o'clock and I used to sit in front of the window with my toy rabbit, waiting for them. That day, I waited and waited but they didn't show. I started to get anxious and asked Jose where they were. He was laying on the couch watching cartoons. He didn't seem too worried. He was more worried about me blocking his view of the TV. Next thing we know, there's a knock on the door. That's when I saw fear on Jose's face. He went to the front door and I followed him. The door burst open and two agents stomped in, dressed in black HAZMAT suits. They grabbed us and I screamed while Jose tried to punch them, but it was hopeless. They threw us in the back of a van and in the blink of an eye, I watched my childhood disappear through that caged window as they drove us away."

Noah's mouth was hanging open and he shut it with a snap. "Who were they?" he breathed.

"Those freaks told us they worked for social services. They told us our parents had been the victims of a terrorist incident at the grocery store. Three Hackers had shown up with infectious symptoms, and they'd coughed their germs all over the store. Our parents had been in direct contact and were taken away by authorities to quarantine. We never saw them again."

The wounds we carry, Noah thought, recalling memories of his mother and his own childhood. "Where were you taken?" he asked quietly.

"St. Joseph's Juvenile Care Facility."

Noah's eyes widened.

"An orphanage," Cecilia said, "but there was nothing religious about it. The building used to be a church and they kept the saint's name for sentimental reasons. Jose and I were dropped off at the front steps with no personal belongings. Just the clothes we were wearing."

Noah shuffled along the crate and put his arm around her shoulder, but she brushed it off. He tried to ignore the pang in his chest.

"Miss Farkas, the Director, met us at the door. She barely even said hello, just led us through the corridors. She was the size of a bull and she barely squeezed between the walls, but she practically blended in with the place, in her smoke-grey HAZMAT suit and all. I'll never forget passing by the occupied bedrooms, and the other children sitting on their beds staring blankly at the walls. It was like their souls had been sucked out of them."

"I didn't think places like that still existed," Noah said, because he needed to say something, anything.

"Oh, they exist, all right. The government doesn't care much for orphans so there are no restrictions on how many children can be housed under one roof. Miss Farkas didn't want a COVID outbreak on her hands though, so she locked us up in individual rooms. I had a bed in one corner, a toilet in the other, and a barred window for ventilation. Meals were brought to us three times a day, if you could call them that. That first winter, my brother caught pneumonia. They told me he didn't survive it. I lived in that prison for six long years . . ." Her voice cracked a little and she looked up at the ceiling. "FLIGHT is an all-inclusive resort compared to where I came from." She turned and looked at him directly. "And that's how I deal with the prospect of never getting out of here."

Noah and Cecilia paused to watch Talia Prinze, a FLIGHT member who often spoke around the virtual bonfire. She was a great orator and Noah enjoyed listening to her, but tonight she was background noise to Cecilia Flores.

"CeCe, you don't have to keep going. It's okay . . ."

"No, I want you to understand who I am, where I come from." She regarded him intently for a moment then looked away. "I remember looking out my barred window one morning. It was a rainy, dreary day. I watched a man enter the orphanage. He told Miss Farkas he wanted to adopt me and two others, which was a rarity at St. Joseph's. She didn't ask him too many questions. The less children she had to feed, the better. We left the orphanage with this man, just like that. He was a wealthy industrialist who traveled often for work and preferred life in isolation. He told us his wife had died before they'd had kids of their own, so he'd decided to adopt. It was his way of tying up broken strings, he said. He lived in a mansion in downtown Toronto, overlooking Lake Ontario. The three of us moved in with him."

"That simple?" Noah said. "What about social services? Legal stuff? Background checks?" It seemed incredible that a guy could just turn up and take three kids away with him. But it was a world Noah hadn't even thought about before, let alone experienced. He suddenly realized how cossetted his life had been.

Cecilia shrugged. "Like I said, the government didn't care about orphans. Anyway, this man called himself Ghost and he encouraged us to call him that too. After we'd been there a couple weeks, he started to push us into academic study. I took an interest in linguistics and he provided the best education money could buy. After studying for a couple years, I started advertising as a tutor in the local newspaper, providing virtual lessons in Spanish, French, German, and Italian."

"Wow," Noah said. "Impressive."

"Not really. But about two years ago, I received an anonymous letter asking to discuss future career opportunities in languages. I had a virtual meeting with someone who interviewed me for a highly-confidential communications job out of the province . . . and they suggested it might not be entirely legal. I brought the subject up with Ghost, and he was hesitant about me taking the job, for obvious reasons. But in the end, he said, 'Life's too short. My dear wife knew that, and I think you know it yourself. Sometimes, you have to take risks, if you don't want to be a prisoner your whole life.' Next thing I knew, I was in Calgary, working here as a communications specialist. Of course, that first anonymous letter was from General Vizor."

Noah nodded. He had a thousand other questions for her, but there was only one he needed to ask now.

"What do you want most in this life, Cecilia Flores?"

She gazed at the star-strewn sky above them for a while. Finally, she turned and looked him straight in the eye.

"The thing I want most in this life, the thing I would do *anything* for, is to have my family back."

Chapter Twenty-One

The next morning, Noah clicked through news articles on the computer at his workstation, but he barely saw them. He felt like he was back in classes. The rest of the team was occupied with their own research.

He sneaked a glance at Cecilia to his left. Her tiny nose was wrinkled as she concentrated on her tablet's screen. Tommy, sitting opposite, noticed and Noah quickly looked back at his screen. He wasn't entirely sure what to make of the feeling in the pit of his stomach when he was around her. Cecilia induced an unknown physiological reaction in him, and he liked it.

"Find anything good?" he asked her at length.

"Not really," she answered. "Prime Minister Talbot's announced a pledge of twenty million dollars for Canada's renewable energy sector, over the next four years."

"Who worries about climate change nowadays? We've got bigger problems, like COVID-37. Right?" he said.

She shrugged.

Tommy huffed a noisy sigh. "You can't be that dim, can you Teslow?" He uncrossed his legs and leaned forward, elbows on the table. "There's an election next year. Talbot's using it to gain the environmentalist vote."

"He's right, you know," Goodwill said from the other end of the table.

"Everything is about appearances in politics," Nikita said.

Viktor grumbled something about distraction without looking up from his work.

"If he really wants votes," Noah said, "he needs to mass-produce the vaccine he's been hiding and end this pandemic. I'm hoping FLIGHT can do that sooner rather than later, so I can forget the name Tommy Chin."

Tommy smirked at him, then looked over at Cecilia. "Hey, Flores," he said. "I want to ask you something."

"What?"

He rolled his chair around the table, elbowing Noah sharply in the ribs along the way, and slid in next to Cecilia. "I keep telling myself to jump into the Simulation Chamber," he said quietly, "but I'm too nervous to try it. I'm more of a tech-guy, you know? I'm not sure how I'd fair in shooting practice."

"Spit it out, Tommy," she said with a smile.

Noah watched more intently than he'd care to admit. He tensed as Tommy leaned closer to Cecilia. "I wonder if you could help me out? I could teach you some coding skills in return. Trade for trade."

"Hm," she said and showed her bright white teeth. "I'll think about it."

Tommy put his arm around Cecilia's shoulders. She didn't brush it away. He grinned at Noah. "I promise it won't be for nothing," he whispered into her ear.

Noah threw his chair back and jumped to his feet. He grabbed Tommy by the neck of his HAZMAT suit and pulled him upright. "That's enough," he said and shoved Tommy backward. Tommy stumbled over his chair's pedestal and fell to the floor.

"Hey!" Cecilia cried and leaped from her own chair. She glanced at Noah through narrowed eyes and squatted next to Tommy. "You alright?"

Tommy nodded and levered himself to his feet. Cecilia stared at Noah, and said, "What's gotten into you?"

Noah failed to meet her eyes. He focused on Tommy instead, who was grinning behind his face-shield. "Oops," he mouthed.

Noah could feel eyes drilling into him from all over the hangar. The rest of the group were on their feet, except for Viktor, who simply shook his head without looking up.

Nikita took a step toward Noah. "Take a walk, kiddo," she said. "To clear your mind. It'll do you some good."

Noah turned on his heels and headed toward the medical bay, where his dad was stationed.

When Noah entered, Eamon was writing something on a clipboard. He glanced over his glasses and lowered his pen when he saw Noah. "Whoa, what's the matter, son?"

Noah realized he was clenching his fists and he forced himself to open his hands. He took a deep breath. "I knocked Tommy Chin down."

"What?"

"I knocked him down."

Eamon frowned. "I don't follow."

"He was pawing Cecilia," Noah said, and the thought of it made him feel sick and angry all over again. "Whispering in her ear, treating her like . . . like, I don't know what."

Eamon stared at him and put his pen in his pocket.

"So, I pulled him off her, and he . . . kind of fell down."

Eamon sighed. "Son, you're going to meet a lot of people in your life who'll upset you or let you down."

"I didn't come here for a lecture."

"Maybe you need one."

Noah crossed his arms and stared at the bare wall.

"Look at me, son. No matter how hard you may try, not everyone will like you. But that's okay. You don't have to like everyone either. You can't champion every person you meet, but you have to learn to make peace with those who cross you."

"I'm trying, Dad, but he makes it so difficult sometimes."

"Try harder. Be the bigger person and walk away."

"I know," he said. "You're right." His dad was always right, even when Noah didn't like it. "I'll try. If not for me, then for FLIGHT."

Chapter Twenty-Two

Muffled conversation filled the cafeteria. Noah sat with his chin on his hand, idly poking his food with a spoon. He peered over at the next table where Tommy and Cecilia were sitting apart from the group, laughing together. The knot in Noah's stomach tightened.

Goodwill, Eamon, and Viktor were heatedly discussing whether NASA would meet its goal to colonize Mars by C75+.

"Personally, I don't see it happening," Eamon said. "The space race is dead. There's nothing to gain financially from exploration into the great beyond."

"You off your rocker, doc?" Goodwill said. "Once we put COVID-37 behind us, our species will repopulate exponentially again. And you know what happens after that—land becomes scarce, the earth becomes polluted, and governments have to find other planets for us to destroy."

Viktor's mouth was downturned. "Terrible to think about moving to new planet, when one we live on gives everything we need. Where did we go wrong?"

"C0+," Eamon said.

The three of them laughed and gathered their food packages from the table. Eamon patted Noah's shoulders on his way back to the medical bay. Noah pulled away from his touch reflexively.

"You doing alright there, kiddo?" Nikita asked. Her red hair was frizzled inside her HAZMAT suit. "Can't help but notice you're upset with Daddy-O."

"I'm fine," he lied.

"You just need to blow off some steam. The Simulation Chamber this afternoon is just what you need. You'll get over this thing. You and your dad seem to get along nicely."

"It's funny, but this is the closest we've ever been. And all it took was becoming fugitives from the government and living out our days in an underground rebel network."

Nikita laughed. "Yup, that'll do it. Look, I don't mean to overstep any boundaries, but what happened with your mom? Not the crazy stepmom, your real mom?"

Noah sighed. "She died, back in C42+. She was only forty. She'd been unwell for months, complaining of bloating and nausea. She wasn't pregnant, so she thought it was some kind of food intolerance. But over the next few months, she started getting more and more tired. She could hardly get out of bed some days. It was hard to see her suffering like that. Dad pleaded with her to see her doctor, but she kept brushing it off."

"That's pretty rough," Nikita said and put her hand over his.

"She finally got medical attention when she developed a cough and fever. Her doctor recommended a COVID-37 swab again and again, which always came back negative. He told her to self-isolate anyway, because it might be a false negative, until she was symptom-free for forty-eight hours."

"But she never became symptom free, did she?" Nikita said.

Noah shook his head. "Things only got worse. She started coughing up blood. Dad was furious with the lack of attention she received from her doctor. After rushing to the ER one day, she was finally given her true diagnosis—ovarian cancer. It had spread to her lungs and liver. She died just a week later. I was eleven years old."

"Oh, honey, I'm so sorry," Nikita said and gripped his hand. "Another unfortunate life lost from our obsession with COVID-37."

"She was the most beautiful and selfless person in the world," Noah said. "She sacrificed her career in biotech research to raise me. Sometimes, I can still smell her perfume, see her smile in my dreams. When she died, Dad closed himself off from everyone, as if emotions can be switched off like a light. He never talked about her death, not even with me. Instead, he used her death as motivation, to design his Distance Band application. I had no idea the whole thing was just a ploy to undermine

OWN and the government." He looked directly into Nikita's open, honest eyes. "I've lived with strangers ever since she died."

"I'm here for you," she said and squeezed his hand again. "You got that, kiddo? And if you get any more trouble from *that*," she jerked her head toward Tommy, "I'm right behind you." She winked and Noah almost smiled.

"Thank you, Nik. I appreciate it." He stared across the tables at Cecilia, who glanced over at him and smiled.

"Hey, life at FLIGHT ain't all that bad," Nikita said and followed his gaze. "When one door closes, another one opens. As the saying goes."

Chapter Twenty-Three

Noah placed his Hover helmet and metal orbs on their respective locker and chest outside the Simulation Chamber.

"Rough day for you, Teslow," Cecilia said as she caught up to him. "You're not usually that far off your game. You're not still bothered by that whole Tommy incident, are you? We all moved past that."

"I didn't sleep well is all. I'm fine," he said and faked a smile.

Ever since coming off Lumox, Noah had found himself navigating wholly unfamiliar emotions. His life before FLIGHT had been bland, with no personal difficulties to help him grow. Even the evening news' negativity hadn't seeped into him—Lumox had kept his emotions at arm's length. Without it, anger, self-doubt, and jealousy had started to brew. He felt like he was spiraling out of control, fighting first with Tommy, then arguing with his dad. His temper seemed to be gaining a mind of its own.

Cecilia gave him a long look before turning away. They headed back to their workstation, where Goodwill and Viktor were focused on their tablets and computers. At the end of the table, General Vizor hovered over Tommy and patted him on the shoulder. Their conversation stopped abruptly when Noah and Cecilia arrived.

"Keep up the good work, Tom," General Vizor said in his raspy tone. "I'm proud of you." He stalked off without a glance at Noah or Cecilia.

Noah's skin crawled at the smug expression on Tommy's face. Since Noah arrived, General Vizor had not made a single attempt to talk with his grandson, and seeing Tommy receive so much attention made Noah loathe his grandfather more.

Cecilia took a seat. "Hey, where are you going?" she said to Noah as he strode away.

"To pay General Vizor an overdue visit."

When he reached the east flank of the hangar, Noah pushed open the steel door to Vizor's office without bothering to knock. He stepped in, as if bracing for a winter storm.

General Vizor was stooped over his mahogany desk, which took up much of the small room. A world map covered the back wall, with colored push pins pressed into different countries. A tall, black metal drawer cabinet was overflowing with papers. On the corner of the desk was a large hourglass, sifting grains of sand, and beside it stood a picture of a young Olivia Teslow. Vizor peered up from the documents scattered across the desktop.

"Who gave you permission to come—"

"Why do you hate me?" Noah blurted out.

The General stood upright but took a step back. "This is why you interrupted me?"

"I'm your grandson," Noah said. He felt his chin trembling. "We're family!" He pointed to the picture of his mother on the desk.

"How dare you bring her up in here," Vizor snarled. "I have no family, not since the day Thea left." A stillness filled the room. The General straightened his navy-blue HAZMAT suit, centering the war medals on his left breast. "Believe it or not, I have no obligation to be a grandfather to you. My only obligation is to FLIGHT, to be a competent leader for those who have placed their trust in me. Toss your childish feelings aside and work for my cause. Or get out."

"I just want to understand why I never heard about you, why you never reached out, even after Mom died."

Vizor sighed. "Take a seat," he said and nodded at the swivel chair in front of his desk. Noah did as he was told and sat awkwardly. "First things first: you never barge in here like this again. Understood?"

Noah nodded.

"Good." Vizor sat and leaned back in his chair. "I've been a fugitive from the government for a long time. When I decided to leave my military post, I knew I would be on the run until my dying day. You can understand why I couldn't just call you at home." He stared at the picture of his daughter. "I've mourned the loss of Olivia with every step I've taken on this Earth, well before she passed away. I lost her when her mother chose to run away from me."

"I can understand why she did, though," Noah said. "She must have felt abandoned."

Vizor stared at him for a long moment and looked as if he might explode. But he took a deep breath and said slowly, "You have no idea what was going on, how much pressure was on me and my department, so don't give me your pop psychology BS. I remember being in my office on Parliament Hill when I was first notified of a rapidly spreading novel coronavirus. We traced the original COVID-19 virus back to Wuhan, in China, to a wet market full of domesticated and wild animals, of all kinds of species."

"The perfect breeding ground," Noah said.

"That's right. China was on course to become the world's new economic and financial superpower in those days. This was a threat to many developed countries, but none more than the United States, which did everything in its power to not only retain world dominance, but to protect democratic nations from the spread of Chinese communism."

Noah looked at the map on the wall; China was covered in red push pins.

"I need you to focus on the bigger picture here," General Vizor said, his stone-black eyes watching Noah like a crow's.

"And what's the bigger picture?"

"You said earlier you wanted to understand. Well, let me enlighten you. Before C0+, the world's leading economic superpowers were Italy, Japan, Germany, France, Canada, the United Kingdom, and the United States of America. Collectively, they were known as the Group of Seven, or more commonly, the G7. The leaders from each country met infrequently to discuss matters ranging from economic crises, the validity of cryptocurrency, global security, and war. China, as an up-and-coming superpower, had been on the G7's radar for years. Many meetings were held behind closed doors with a select few elite members, to discuss how best to deal with the threat of China. Ideas were pitched but the seven members couldn't agree upon any."

Vizor reached into a drawer and rummaged around in it. "One summer morning, in June of 2019, the US president and his advisors devised a plot to eliminate China once and for all. He called a covert G7 meeting that same month to outline a timeline of events to establish ongoing world dominance. The plan was called 'The Great Reset'."

"The Great Reset," Noah repeated dully.

"Here," Vizor said and slid a flexi-glass tablet across the desk. "Read it."

The top of the screen read:

CLASSIFIED

The Great Reset

1. Lead scientists will work in a top-secret lab, developing a man-made deadly virus strain that is more easily communicable and fatal than any other known virus.

2. This man-made virus will be secretly hand-delivered to a wet market in China where occult inoculation to different animal species will occur, in an environment so feasible to conceive a novel virus that the public would not question it.

3. Animal-to-human transmission of the novel virus will take place and rapidly spread worldwide, with gain of function mutations producing variants of the virus more deadly than the last, creating a global pandemic equating to global chaos, killing millions in its wake.

4. Each country's government will try to restore order from the ensuing chaos and recommend public health orders including, but not limited to, self-isolation at home, washing and sanitizing hands, wearing masks, and staying six feet apart if needing to venture out into public spaces.

5. With enough time, the collective human spirit will falter in its hopes of eliminating the novel virus—with enough human deaths, along with an economic depression the likes of which has never been seen, the world will point its finger at the country responsible for the disaster—China.

6. Harnessing the natural human desire for vengeance, the leaders of G7 countries will rally the support of other countries to bring down China, crippling the country as a threat once and for all.

7. The G7 countries, under the direction of the United States of America, will continue to lead the globe through a never-ending pandemic, controlling the masses and remaining in power indefinitely.

Noah looked up from the tablet. His throat was constricted, and he felt his mouth hanging open, though he lacked the wit to close it. He wasn't sure if he was even breathing, but he must have been, for eventually, he said, "Does everyone here know about this?"

"Only those I actively recruited. In other words, everyone but you. As I said, you need to start focusing on the bigger picture."

"Why haven't you released this to the public?" Noah asked, readjusting in his seat. "Wouldn't this be enough to take down the G7?"

"It's not an original—there's no official government signatures," he pointed to the bottom of the digitized document. "Anyone reading this would deem it nothing more than conspiracy. We need legitimate proof to make our stand."

Noah nodded. "So, how exactly did the G7 cause China to fall?"

"Well, not every G7 leader was on board with The Great Reset. Germany and Japan were strongly opposed, afraid of repeating the mistakes of World War Two. But in the end, both countries were coerced to accept the plan, which was carried out in November of 2019."

"C0+," Noah said.

General Vizor nodded.

"And you went along with it?" Noah asked.

"I was told half-truths by our Prime Minister of the time. The true nature of COVID-19's origins and China's involvement—or lack thereof—were veiled in secrecy. In C7+, under the direction of the G7 and OWN Industries, myself and other world military leaders were put on standby for a nuclear assault on China, should they not accept responsibility for COVID-19."

"That is insane," Noah said. "The G7 was willing to risk World War Three?"

"Yes," General Vizor said, frowning. "I'm still coming to grips with it myself. The Great Reset weighs heavily on me, even now. I dedicated my whole life to serving and protecting my country, which in the end, was lying to me. To us all."

General Vizor turned his back on Noah, facing the world map on the wall.

"How did you find out about it?" Noah asked.

"The truth always leaks out, no matter how tight the seal. Information trickled down from contacts within the government, though none made it out into the public domain."

"OWN controls the news media," Noah said and felt like slapping his forehead at his lack of vision. "They've kept it hidden all this time to fit their agenda." It was all so obvious, now that it had been spelled out to him.

"Now you're seeing the bigger picture," Vizor said approvingly, turning back around.

"But what about China?"

"World leaders demanded that China pay reparations to every country for the enormous loss of life and economy. Sanctions were rigorously enforced and the Chinese government had no choice but to agree. They folded like a house of cards. The Great Reset was complete."

Chapter Twenty-Four

Twenty-four hours later, Noah flattened his back against the wall of a shadowed alleyway in a computer-generated city. On his face-shield's heads-up display, his vital signs were raised but healthy, and his drone kill was twenty. He glanced over his right shoulder and saw Cecilia in an alleyway across the street.

"What's your count?" she hollered.

"Twenty! You?"

"You gotta do better than that! I'm at twenty-six!"

Although this was an entirely simulated experience, Noah knew it wasn't without its risks; the drones couldn't physically harm anyone, but the weapons the trainees carried could, if they weren't careful—which was why they all had to watch a safety video before entering the Simulation Chamber.

Noah heard the buzzing of approaching drones, accurately recreated in his helmet's HD surround sound speaker array.

"Five drones coming our way!" he shouted.

Cecilia grinned. "Game on."

They both ducked along the length of their alleys toward each other, bubble shields raised as they scanned the sky. Twenty meters away, five black and white drones raced toward them. Their cameras and cannons swiveled toward the alleys. Noah and Cecilia aimed their phase-shift guns, but before they could fire, five energy blasts hit each drone squarely in an explosion of metal debris.

"What the—?"

Noah spun around but no one was there. He looked across the deserted street at Cecilia, who stared back at him bemused.

"Gotta be quicker than that, kiddos!"

Nikita strode up the middle of the street swinging her gun nonchalantly. "Five more kills. That takes me up to forty-seven."

"Those were ours," Cecilia moaned.

Nikita raised a gloved hand and started counting on her fingers. "Hold on a minute, I need to do some quick math." She furrowed her brow and stuck her tongue out of the corner of her mouth. "Yep, I still beat your combined kills. Better luck next time." She winked at Noah.

He rolled his eyes. "You beat us by one kill. Don't let it go to your head."

The trio scanned the skies but there were no drones in sight, so they deactivated their shields and guns, which retracted into their orbs.

"You ever think about the old days, Nik?" Cecilia said. "Before the drones took over?"

"Only every night. Why do you ask?"

Cecilia shrugged. "Just curious to hear the other side of things. From someone who lived through the changes from human to machine."

"Things were always ugly on the Force," Nikita said. "But they got especially bad from C0+ to C2+. Police brutality was in the headlines every week. The evidence was impossible to ignore and something needed to change."

Noah nodded. "My grandparents told me the story of George Floyd once," he said. "You can say what you like about police drones, but at least they aren't programmed to asphyxiate people. It's a horrible story. They had him pinned down for almost nine full minutes."

"I remember sitting in my cruiser on Queen Street when George's story broke," Nikita said. "His death was as widespread on the news as COVID itself. It brought about its own revolution. Made people realize they had to change systemic racism and police brutality."

Noah recalled the stories. People all over the world had taken to the streets, sick and tired of the unfair and unjust systems of the law. Unfortunately, the revolt had occurred during the initial stages of the global pandemic, which forced politicians to perform a delicate balancing act: they had to promote self-isolation to curb COVID-19 transmission, while allowing freedom of speech and peaceful protests.

Nikita said, "It's a shame those Distance Bands rolled out in C2+ like they did. As if things weren't bad enough, the government enforced safety over freedom. It killed the marches. The names were all silenced."

"But the protests obviously made a difference," Cecilia said. "The Defund the Police movement *did* happen."

"Yeah, it sure did. The police chiefs heard the demonstrators loud and clear. They replaced one devil with another."

They walked in silence for a moment. "A working group at the top level held meetings to create a new system of policing," Nikita said eventually. "One that would phase out humans in place of police drones over several years. The first drone joined our team in C3+ and as its technology became more and more sophisticated, human errors and biases were eliminated."

She stopped abruptly. Noah walked into Cecilia who gave him an exasperated look. He held up his hands sheepishly.

Nikita turned to face them. "Now, I'm all for improving the system, but you tell me, did anyone think about the decent officers who were robbed of their work because they were no longer deemed essential?" Her voice was quivering, though Noah wasn't sure if it was with anger, regret, or both. "All because of a few bad apples? Did police brutality really stop or did we just substitute human brutality with machine brutality?" She closed her eyes and drew in a deep breath. "Sorry, kiddos.

I've stored a lot of my past deep inside me. About time I let it out of the vault." She turned and walked on.

"Nik," Noah said cautiously. "Can I ask you something?"

"Shoot."

"Why did the police department get rid of you? I mean, I hear what you said about police drones replacing you guys, but there must've been some other role for you. I'm sure you're made of more than just your sharpshooting skills."

"They didn't get rid of me. I quit."

"Quit?" he said as he stepped over a pile of rubble. "Why?"

"The world isn't fair," she replied somberly. "But I guess you've realized that by now." She cleared her throat and regarded Noah levelly. "Back in Toronto—a couple years before the pandemic started—I was the Academy's poster girl. The brass trusted me, and my colleagues respected me, both in and out of the line of duty. I could handle myself." She smiled ruefully. "Things were going great, career-wise."

They entered a park surrounded by skyscrapers. The sun was shining on perfectly trimmed grass.

"My dating life was non-existent," Nikita went on, "which didn't bother me in my early years, but the older I got, the more I romanticized about settling down. I tried dating apps, but I couldn't find any quality men there. Then, one morning before a shift, I was standing in line at the local coffee shop, waiting to place my order. A guy called Vance Jones who I made regular small-talk with each morning bought my coffee that day. I had some time to kill, so we sat and chatted. We went on a few more dates and we ended up falling in love." She flushed and Noah realized that she wasn't as comfortable talking about her life as she wanted them to believe. "After six months, he moved in with me. He worked for the railway company, and eventually he was rotated onto nightshift, which really screwed up his sleep schedule and made him pretty irritable over the smallest things. When COVID-19 hit, he was laid off and his mental health deteriorated. I was there for him, of course, but it was a really hard time for both of us. I couldn't be around all the time caring for him. I became the sole earner. Someone had to pay the rent."

They stepped onto a stone bridge over a lake and sat on the low wall. Noah looked at his reflection in the still water, as if he were looking in a mirror. Below the surface, he sensed movement.

"My grandparents told me how difficult those early years were," he said simply.

"Well, it got worse," Nikita replied. "I still had my job, but it was becoming more trouble than it was worth. Because of COVID-19, we had new safety protocols to follow. And as if that wasn't enough, we also had to do our jobs effectively alongside those newly operational police drones."

"It must've been tough," Cecilia said.

"It was. One evening, my partner and I got a distress call at a downtown block near my place. A man in his late twenties was suicidal and deemed a threat to the public. We sped over there right away. The drones always beat us to the scene, of course, avoiding traffic lights and taking shortcuts. But when we got there, I realized the call was in my apartment complex. I rushed inside and up the stairs, terrified that someone had harmed my Vance. And sure enough, the commotion was in my apartment. The door was already wide open and my poor Vance was on the floor in a pool of blood. He had multiple gunshot wounds to the chest—caused by the three attending police drones. Another simple mental health check gone wrong."

She hung her head and Noah had an urge to put his arm around her, which he resisted. He didn't know if his consolation would be welcome. There was so much he didn't know about real human interaction.

"I lost my mind," Nikita said. "I pulled out my gun and blasted each drone until they lay on the floor as lifeless as my sweet Vance. Our duty was to serve and protect but the drones were more lethal to the public than any corrupt police officer on the streets. I drove back to the station, and left my gun and badge on the Captain's desk without a word."

Cecilia glanced briefly at her and looked away again before speaking. "Thank you for sharing with us, Nik. We've all lost so much." She looked across the lake thoughtfully.

"Life goes on," Nikita said quietly.

Noah kept his gaze down on the lake. Nothing he said would've been adequate; compared to the people he'd met at FLIGHT, he'd lived a cosseted, sheltered life.

Beneath the bridge, the water started to ripple. Without warning, a swarm of drones shot up into the sky from the depths of the lake, creating a fountain effect. Noah, Cecilia, and Nikita dropped to the ground as the drones opened fire. The bridge's low wall shielded them, but bits of brick and dust pinged off in all directions as the drones' artillery gradually destroyed it.

Noah activated his orbs and stood up, shield raised. He blasted away at the drones as Nikita and Cecilia followed his lead. It didn't take long for them to clear the skies, but for once, Noah took no pleasure in it. None of them bothered to brag about their kill count. Nikita's story had drained the exercise of enjoyment.

Noah's Hover helmet flashed *SIMULATION COMPLETE* and all around him, the city disintegrated in a blur of green pixels, reverting back into a room with reflective panelling. They all took off their helmets, walked back along the short corridor to the Disinfectant Chamber and out into the main hangar.

Nikita placed her orbs in the chest and helmet in the locker. "I'm gonna take a quick stroll around," she said. "I need to clear my head a bit. I'll see you kiddos later." Her face was pale, emphasizing her red hair. She turned and walked away, waving over her shoulder.

Noah frowned as he put his orbs back. He looked at Cecilia and said, "C'mon, let's see what the rest of the team has been up to."

They strolled through the hangar toward their table, but everyone was huddled together at the western wall, talking and gesturing animatedly.

"What in the world is going on?" Cecilia said.

They weaved through the empty tables and chairs until they reached the crowd. They pushed their way through the bodies, as someone shouted, "He did it!"

They broke into the center of the crowd and bumped into Goodwill. "CeCe, Noah! We were wondering when you two would show up. Eamon just went looking for you guys. You missed all the action." He gestured to his right, where Tommy Chin stood with his arms folded. Tommy didn't acknowledge their arrival but he was smirking.

"What's all the fuss about?" Noah said. "What did we miss?"

"You won't believe it—the bloody Russian just cracked the code!" Goodwill cried.

On the other side of the crowd, Viktor sat in front of his computer punching the air. A group of people suddenly lifted his chair above their shoulders and Viktor's grey bushy brows arched as they carried him forward. "Viktor-y!" they chanted. "Viktor-y! Viktor-y!"

"Did he really—?" Noah's voice failed him.

"Yes, Viktor isolated the spike protein," Goodwill said and seemed unable to control the grin that was engulfing his face. "A COVID-37 vaccine is finally on the horizon!"

Noah grabbed Cecilia and hugged her tightly. Without thinking, he flipped up his face-shield. She did the same.

He closed his eyes and kissed her soft lips.

Chapter Twenty-Five

Noah eyes widened when he realized what he was doing. *Don't panic,* he thought. He separated his lips from hers and held her by her shoulders.

"You alright, Teslow?" Cecilia said.

"Yeah. Yeah, I'm good."

"Then why do you have that look on your face?"

Noah's heart beat harder. "I have to go." He quickly turned and walked into the crowd.

You're panicking, you idiot.

He looked over his shoulder and Cecilia stood with her hands on her hips shaking her head.

Noah grabbed a bottle of vodka from a crate of alcohol that Vizor and his advisors retrieved from his office. He took a long swig and grimaced. He ran into other members seated at worktables, their arms over each other's shoulders swaying and singing, 'For he's a jolly good fellow'. Noah joined and drank some more.

General Vizor marched into the half-circle and everyone went quiet. He stood there for a moment staring at the group. "Well? Are you just going to stand there looking like buffoons or are we going to celebrate?" He smiled which caused everyone to recoil at the unusual sight. Vizor passed bottles of Scotch whiskey around and sung songs with the rest of the group.

Fifteen minutes later, Noah broke off and stumbled into Goodwill who sat on top of an empty table laughing wholeheartedly at passers-by and slapping his knees.

"How's it going, Goodwill?"

There was a half-empty bottle of rum next to him and he gave Noah a big hug.

"Been here a long time, boy. You don't know what this good news means to me, to my soul. Come on, take a seat." He patted the empty chair next to him.

"I'm happy for you, Goodwill," Noah said and collapsed onto the chair. He swigged the vodka. "I'm happy for all of us." Goodwill was one of the good guys. "Can I tell you a secret?"

"Sure thing. Go on now."

"I lost my Cross," Noah murmured.

"Your what?"

"My Cross. It was a birthday gift from my dad. I had it with me the night we drove to Calgary. I don't have the nerve to tell him I lost it." He chewed his lip.

Goodwill threw his head back and laughed. "What's it to your father, anyhow? Haven't you heard, boy? Religion is dead. Been that way for decades."

Noah smiled uneasily. "I know, but I think it was for something important. My dad's side of the family were practicing Catholics. At least they were, pre-COVID."

"Let me fill you in on a little secret of my own," Goodwill whispered. "My brother Theodore was a *priest* back in his heyday. You ever met someone who was a priest?"

Noah shook his head, which made the room spin. "Never. My Grandma Noelle and Grandpa John were devout Catholics, so they used to talk about priests. I think their religion really helped them, especially during the pandemic."

"No doubt."

"Dad isn't much of a believer. In fact, he's an atheist. Sometimes I wonder if he would've handled Mom's death better if he'd believed in God."

"It would do a lot of people good to believe in something."

"Cheers to that," Noah said and they clinked bottles. He slugged more vodka and grimaced again as it burned his throat.

"My brother Theo," Goodwill said, "he used to preach inside those historical buildings, churches, not sure how familiar you are with them. They disappeared long before your time. When COVID-19 hit, Theo and many of his brothers went virtual, as if they had a choice—social gatherings of any kind were banned, including attendance at church. Most priests followed the restrictions, but some didn't."

"It's always the few that ruin it for the many," Noah said into his bottle.

"Ain't that the truth. I remember Theo being so angry at those that continued to congregate, like they were immune to the plague."

Noah slumped back in his chair. "My grandparents used to love going to church. Tell me more about what happened."

Goodwill collected his thoughts. "The law-breaking priests sent weekly underground invites to local believers, to attend Mass. The Christian faith wasn't unique in this, boy. Other faiths had their own places of worship: mosques, temples, synagogues, and so on. Their holy leaders found ways to hold underground gatherings too. You can guess what happened next."

"The underground worshippers caught COVID."

"Oh, please," Goodwill said and flicked his hand at Noah. "It spread like *wildfire*. Many of the faithful perished. Those who survived resolved that their God was needed more than ever to unite them against this terrible disease. Again, you may be too young to remember, but Distance Bands were rolled out at the beginning of C2+. Many were uncertain exactly how they worked, and others completely ignored them. The faithful wondered whether the bands were a government ploy to create fear and cripple the masses."

"They didn't stop gathering, did they?" Noah said.

He knew firsthand the severe penalties that came with disobeying Distance Band rules.

"You bet they didn't. The God-praising, law-breaking devotees continued to worship underground with congregations maintaining the appropriate two-meter distance between each other to remain undetected. But the government was smarter than that; they planted undercover informants to report on these underground religious flocks. One by one, the worshippers disappeared. By C7+, all organized religious activities were punishable by death."

"And your brother Theo? What happened to him?"

"The poor fool passionately bore the Cross all the way to his grave."

Noah ditched his bottle on the table. "Well, that's depressing."

"Life's dark, ain't it? That's why we're here, boy. To take back what's ours. The government seized control of our freedom and religion, all for the 'greater good'. They argued that cruel measures were needed to stop further spread of COVID-19 and its variants. Now, I ain't no bimbo—I understood the government's logic—but how was my brother, and those others so deeply committed to their faith, supposed to fare against the hardships of isolation? How were they supposed to protect themselves against a world descending into hell?"

Goodwill wagged his finger at Noah and adopted a deeply resonant, authoritarian voice. "You have your antidepressants," he intoned. "That will save you."

Chapter Twenty-Six

The alarm sounded at 6 a.m. Noah jolted up in his top bunk with a pounding headache. He peered down at the vacant lower bunk; his dad was already up. For a minute, he had to convince himself that last night hadn't been a dream. Viktor Ivanov had isolated the spike protein of the COVID-37 virus, effectively discovering the secret weapon in their fight against the man-made pandemic. The atmosphere inside the hangar had become electric; everyone at FLIGHT was suddenly much more hopeful for the future. But Noah knew there was still a mountain of questions to address.

Who might produce the vaccine? Could FLIGHT go public without government or OWN retribution? How could the vaccine be fairly distributed? Would the general population even accept a vaccine from an anti-government organization—one that the media had already labeled as terrorists?

Noah climbed out of his bunker and padded to the dorm bathroom. On his way back out, he bumped into Cecilia, whose hair was frazzled inside her red HAZMAT suit. Noah blushed; he'd spent the night in bed thinking about their kiss and how he embarrassed himself by walking away from it. He wondered what she thought about last night. After all, she was the first girl he had ever kissed.

"Morning, CeCe," he said in the most macho voice he could muster.

"Good morning, stranger," she said and yawned. "That was quite a celebration last night. I got a pounding headache this morning. I wonder how Goodwill's doing."

Noah smiled. "Last I saw, he was passed out by a stack of empty pizza boxes near the kitchen. I talked to him for a while. He kept hugging me. And anybody else who got close enough."

Cecilia bit her lip. "He's due to make that public address to our underground listeners today. I hope he's recovered enough to share the good news."

Noah and Cecilia reached the bustling cafeteria, making their way to the counter for a breakfast packed with eggs, bacon, and potatoes. They found a table and Eamon joined them.

"Morning, son. Morning, CeCe. Glad to see you're both absent from the patient observation units, unlike some." He laughed. "Been a busy morning for alcohol detox."

As they started to eat, outside the cafeteria General Vizor stepped up to a podium with two of his advisors, Paul Colleaux and George Nibien. He was back to his stoic demeanor after last night's loss of inhibitions. His stone-black eyes scanned the crowd around the podium and those in the cafeteria.

"Last night was a cause for celebration," he said. "I am incredibly proud of what we've all accomplished here, but special thanks are due to Viktor Ivanov. Join me in giving him another round of applause."

The whole hangar erupted in claps and cheers. Viktor was leaning against the cafeteria counter and he produced a half-smile, raising his hand in acknowledgment.

General Vizor continued. "Despite this major breakthrough, our destination is far from reached. Moving forward, our first order of business will be to try and find a pharmaceutical company willing to invest in a COVID-37 vaccine under covert conditions. This will not be an easy task. Our second priority is to coordinate our efforts with satellite FLIGHT networks across the country to decipher government documents. The truth of the pandemic must be known to all. Change starts with ripple effects. I want our media and communications specialists to inform our underground listeners that we have reached a tipping point." He paused to look out to the crowd. His gaze landed on Noah and Eamon as he said, "I trust that everyone understands the significance of our efforts. If anyone sees or hears of any plans that may jeopardize our operations, speak to me directly."

Noah felt the sting of the words but bit down on his anger. This was no time for dissent, with victory in their sights. So, he kept his peace and locked eyes with Vizor.

Eventually, the General looked away. "As you all know, in the next few days we will enter C50+. Countries around the world will commemorate this milestone in different ways and on different dates, but the Canadian government has chosen the first of July to pay tribute to Canada Day, our historic national holiday. There will be a large celebration at the front steps of parliament in Ottawa, broadcasting live on TV. FLIGHT will hijack the event to broadcast our message of truth." The crowd stared at him silently. "Now, does anyone have any questions? No? Good. Back to your work, then." He stepped down from the podium and stalked away.

Noah, Cecilia, and Eamon looked at each other. Eamon shrugged and they continued with their breakfasts.

Back at their workstation, Noah said, "Well, it was good to see General Vizor back to his old self."

The three of them laughed as Goodwill joined them at the table.

"Morning, Goodwill. How are you feeling?" Eamon said.

"Like a million bucks, doc. Thanks to that quick detox program you guys got running in the back." He chuckled. "Boy, let me tell you, I haven't drunk like that in years and I don't miss it one bit." He gathered bits of audio equipment from his end of the table and started plugging little black boxes into other little black boxes. Noah had no idea what any of them were. "Let me get my microphone set up here."

"Microphone?" Noah said as Goodwill produced a huge metal tube with a black mesh half-dome on one end and a thick wire trailing from the other.

"Goodwill is the voice of FLIGHT," Cecilia said. "He's the man our underground audience hears when they tune in."

"I sure am," Goodwill said and flashed his toothy smile. "My mind is clear and I'm ready to get this show on the road. CeCe, you ready?"

"Am I ever not ready?" Cecilia said. "Just hand me your script and I'll translate it."

"It seems crazy to me that you can broadcast to the whole world from this table," Noah said with genuine awe.

"You better believe it," Goodwill said. "Thanks to CeCe and her linguistic pals, we got listeners all over Europe and Asia."

"The frequency isn't public knowledge," Cecilia said. "Most of our listeners are FLIGHT supporters working silently from home. Some of them are too nervous to abandon their families and join us, or they're too scared of government punishment if they get caught." She pulled a coil of wire from a rack and handed it to Noah. "Now, make yourself useful and plug one end of this into the top amp in that rack over there."

By the time they'd finished setting up the amplifiers, transmitters, mics, and mixing desk, it was mid-morning. Over the past few weeks, while Noah hadn't had anything to do with audio gear, he had learned how to uplink the outputs from Goodwill's desk and rack-mounted equipment to the high-bandwidth fiber line, which sent the encoded signal to the transmitter, located atop a hill forty miles south.

With everything ready to go, Goodwill was seated comfortably on one end of the table with his microphone in a shock-mount cradle in front of him, with Cecilia sitting opposite him. Eamon, who oversaw the broadcast, pointed at Noah, who clicked on various switches arranged on his screen's virtual soundboard. They all turned green as they accepted their inputs, and when he clicked on the uplink button, he pointed at Goodwill.

"Good morning, listeners," Goodwill said in his finest, honey-rich broadcast voice. "This is your friend and the voice of reason, Goodwill, coming at you live on Thursday, December twenty-sixth, C49+. We have a *very* special message for you today. Here at FLIGHT, we've made great strides in our fight against the government and OWN Industries. Just last night, we decoded the spike protein for COVID-37, no mean feat with the government keeping the virus' genetic data locked up. We are now one step closer to a cure for this man-made catastrophe."

Goodwill was in his element; he spoke with passion, gesticulating radiantly even though his listeners couldn't see him. His dark, translucent eyes flashed like cold fire. He spoke for another twenty-five minutes before wrapping up.

"That's all I have for you today, fellow truth seekers. I'll bring you updates on our progress over the coming months but for now, I ask that you stand back and stand by."

He paused and grinned at his mic. "A tsunami is coming."

Chapter Twenty-Seven

High above the ceiling of FLIGHT's hangar, Noah watched the seasons change. The cold winter melted into a wet spring then a sunny summer. No one could leave the hangar in case they were spotted by the authorities, so the natural light from the glass ceiling was all that kept cabin fever at bay.

In January of C50+, General Vizor contacted a representative from a small pharmaceutical company in Ontario called Mesiha&Co. The company was on the verge of bankruptcy, unable to compete with the giant drug companies that dominated the market. The General convinced Mesiha&Co that FLIGHT's vaccine would not only make them the new leaders in the drug industry, but also cement their name into future history books. Going up against the government and OWN Industries caused Mesiha&Co's board more than a few sleepless nights, but after intense negotiations, they agreed to work on a COVID-37 vaccine with FLIGHT.

The plan was to launch it only after the government and its corrupt institutions were exposed and brought down.

By June C50+— seven months after Noah and Eamon arrived here—vaccine development operations were running smoothly. Once Viktor had isolated the spike protein, everything started weaving together.

Despite the success of the research though, things at FLIGHT became increasingly tense. July 1st was approaching quickly and the redacted government documents obtained by Tommy were still not deciphered. Before Vizor could go live in front of the nation, he needed evidence of The Great Reset; no one would believe a fugitive without hard proof, and plenty of it. Every team worked around the clock to try and break the code.

On June 27th, the documents were finally broken. There were a plethora of research papers among them, explaining the development of the man-made COVID-19 virus, and numerous studies on its transmissibility and virulence. There were detailed records highlighting every step of The Great Reset, signed by world leaders of the time, linking all of the G7 countries to its plans. It was exactly the proof Vizor needed.

The government was on high alert for terrorist threats on Canada Day. The spectacle was to be broadcast all over Canada and the world. A parade would start the day, through the empty streets of Ottawa while guest speakers paid homage to the government and its affiliate organizations. Enormous and awe-inspiring firework displays were planned, and finally, Prime Minister Gregoire Talbot would give a speech before the cameras, thanking everyone for containing COVID-37 and feeding the propaganda machine.

Security for the event was unprecedented. Drones were already patrolling the streets and skies, and cybersecurity had been greatly ramped up. Thankfully, FLIGHT had Tommy Chin, who breached firewalls like they were made of Lego. He was in charge of hacking government databases and seizing control of the broadcast transmissions. General Vizor would then override the Prime Minister's speech to deliver his own to the world audience. The whole operation couldn't happen without Tommy, and General Vizor trusted him without reservation. Tommy would load the gun and Vizor would fire it.

General Vizor dubbed his plan The Great Restart.

Chapter Twenty-Eight

As he geared himself up for tomorrow's Great Restart operation, Noah imagined that one of two scenarios would play out once the world heard the truth about the COVID virus. Either the global community would wake up and revolt, taking back its freedom—or it would go into even deeper denial and continue to swallow the government's lies. He was afraid to think what might happen if it were the latter.

Although Noah had always known his time with FLIGHT wasn't permanent, a big part of him was going to miss it when everything was over. He'd made a lot of new friends here and for the first time in his life, he truly felt a connection to others. But if FLIGHT was successful in carrying out The Great Restart, what would happen next? Would he move back to Saskatoon with his dad? Who would replace the government if it toppled? Would there be enough vaccine for the whole world?

Would Cecilia still be in his life?

He glanced up at the team, busily occupied around the big table; only Eamon was absent, working in the medical bay. These people were his friends, and he was going to miss them.

"Hey Nik," he said impulsively. "You up for joining CeCe and me after lunch in the Simulation Chamber? One last time, so I beat your record."

Tommy lounged back in his chair with his feet up on the corner of the table. He sneered as he chewed gum. "You're still training even though the big launch is tomorrow? I hate to break it to you, but you've been wasting your time."

"I've been training just like General Vizor told us," Noah snapped. "Who knows what's coming? I hope you'll be able to handle a gun and shield, if it comes to that."

"Don't worry about me, chum. I've made it this far, and the way I see it, FLIGHT would be nothing without me. You know it, your dad knows it, and General Vizor knows it. Without the documents I secured, FLIGHT would still be in the Dark Ages. I don't need to train for any upcoming threats. The new world will be here in twenty-four hours and it's all because of me." He blew his gum into a bubble until it popped.

"Hey, Tomboy," Nikita said and stood up. She glared at Tommy and clenched her fists. "Your head looks a little full. Need me to punch some of that ego out to bring you back down to Earth with the rest of us?"

Goodwill grabbed Nikita's arm and pulled her back into her seat. Viktor barely peered up from his work.

Tommy gave her a dark look. "Truth hurts, doesn't it?"

"Just ignore him," Noah said. "He's just trying to get under our skin. The guy hasn't done anything useful since he's been here." There was a hostility to him that Noah hated.

"You got something to say to me, tough guy?" Tommy was on his feet now. He stepped up to Noah until his face-shield was right in front of Noah's.

Noah didn't flinch. "You've been nothing but a thorn in my side ever since I met you. If you had any worth, you'd come into the Simulation Chamber with us and show us you're a part of this team."

Tommy gritted his teeth.

"Didn't think so," Noah said.

Cecilia put a hand on Noah's shoulder. "C'mon Noah, let's grab lunch. After tomorrow, you don't have to see his face ever again." She shot Tommy a fake smile.

Everyone but Tommy stood and headed for the cafeteria.

"Man, that Tomboy must hold the world's record for the longest streak of waking up on the wrong side of the bed," Nikita said.

"Don't be quick to judgment of young fellow," Viktor said, which made everybody turn and stare at him.

Goodwill laughed. "Viktor! You found your voice again!"

"What are you going on about, Vikky?" Nikita said.

Viktor harrumphed at her pet name for him. "Any of you speak with Tommy to understand why he angry all time?"

Nobody said anything, but they all looked away awkwardly as they reached the cafeteria counter. They grabbed their lunches and made their way over to a vacant table.

"Well," Cecilia said hesitantly. "No. Not really. Have you, Viktor?"

"Of course not," Viktor said. "But I read his FLIGHT profile."

"FLIGHT profile?" Noah said. "We have access to profiles?"

"You don't," Viktor said as he pulled out his portable tablet. "But I am special privilege. I'm not supposed to share, but last day at FLIGHT, no damage to be done."

He clicked on an app and put the screen in the middle of the table for everyone to see. Tommy Chin's profile picture was on the left with a description of him.

The group huddled around to read it.

Name:	*Tommy (Huo) Chin*
Age:	*24*
Sex:	*Male*
Race:	*Oriental-Caucasian*
Place of Birth:	*Vancouver, B.C., Canada*
Weight:	*155 lbs*
Height:	*5'10"*

Tommy (Huo) Chin was raised by his mother, Sylvia Burrow from Vancouver, B.C., and his father Li Chin, a previous government official who immigrated from Wuhan, China in C0+. A single child, he excelled in music, art, and computer programming at an early age and was placed in prestigious schools. Aged eight, he was witness to his parents' murder inside their suburban home; unbeknownst to him, his father had provided intelligence on the Chinese government to the G7. The gunmen belonged to the Mercenaries of the Old Republic.

Tommy was forced into a foster home, where he developed significant anxiety issues. He transferred from one home to another due to increasingly erratic behavior— destruction of property, violation of COVID restrictions, emotional dysregulation, and altercations with his peers. He was eventually admitted to a child psychiatry unit, and diagnosed with PTSD, Conduct Disorder, and Oppositional Defiant Disorder. He was heavily medicated and underwent intensive psychotherapy. He remained problematic in the foster care system, until he reached the age of eighteen, at which point he was discharged to fend for himself.

He perfected the art of theft and deceit while living on the streets for two years, until he saved enough money to

*enroll himself into the University of BC to pursue a
computer science major.*

Things suddenly made a lot more sense to Noah, even though he
found he still didn't like Tommy. He looked up at the rest of the group and
they all seemed to be feeling as guilty as Noah was.

Cecilia asked the question that had sprung to Noah's mind.
"What's this about the 'Mercenaries of the Old Republic'?"

Viktor leaned in and whispered, "There exists network of
nationalists belonging to Old Republic of China. They work in shadows,
like FLIGHT. The Mercenaries rose from destruction of their government
by The Great Reset operation. They have assassins across globe. Tommy's
parents were killed by Mercenaries to avenge betrayal of homeland."

"Tommy doesn't know any of this?" Noah said.

"He knows none of it," Eamon said from behind Noah. He
snatched the tablet. "And he never will."

Chapter Twenty-Nine

After lunch, Cecilia, Nikita, and Noah left Eamon, Goodwill, and Viktor. They headed to the Simulation Chamber but none of them mentioned Tommy Chin. Noah knew they'd overstepped their boundaries in reading his personal history.

When Nikita entered the chamber, Noah held Cecilia back. "I don't feel right about reading what we just did."

"I don't either," she said. "But what's there to do about it?"

"We've got to keep it from Tommy. Jeez, I'm not good in these situations."

Cecilia smirked. "Follow my lead. I'm a natural at these things, growing up in an orphanage and all."

Somehow, she always seemed to put him at ease. He said, "That whole thing about Tommy's parents being killed, you think that has anything to do with why he never goes into the Simulation Chamber?"

"Maybe. Perhaps he's just protecting himself from childhood trauma. Never thought about that."

"My whole life had been a lie up until I joined FLIGHT," Noah said regretfully. "My dad and Jasmine were spies on opposite sides, while the government lied about COVID."

"And your point is?"

"I would've appreciated my dad not leaving me in the dark for so long." He regarded her for a long time before saying, "I'm going to tell Tommy about his parents next time I see him. He deserves that, at least."

Cecilia's eyes sparkled. "I'm in. We'll tell him together, when the time is right. We can save someone else from their pain, if nothing else. I'd kill to know what happened to my parents."

Noah nodded. "If I hadn't left my house that winter night, I'd still be trapped in my old routines. I'd still be oblivious to what's really going on in the world."

"Ignorance is bliss for some," Cecilia said.

"Not for me. The truth is important, no matter how uncomfortable it is. Leaving was the best decision I ever made. I found my family. I found my purpose. I found myself."

I found you, he wanted to say but clamped his jaw shut before he could make a fool of himself.

He was going to miss Cecilia. She wasn't just his training buddy— he was reluctant to admit it even to himself, but she was also his first love. And he was sure she felt the same. He was comfortable with her whether they were talking, goofing off, or just sitting in silence. He'd felt a pressure building up inside him for the last couple of weeks, and he badly needed to ask her what plans she had for when FLIGHT dissolved. But the moment never felt right.

We'll cross that bridge once we get there, he told himself.

They grabbed their orbs and helmets and entered the Simulation Chamber, where Nikita was waiting for them.

"Well, look who decided to finally show up," she said. "Ready for our last round? Gonna miss whopping you, kiddos."

"We're gonna miss you too, Nik," Noah said.

"You've come a long way since you got here," Nikita said.

"That feels like a lifetime ago. I swear I've matured more in the past seven months than the last seven years."

He glanced over at Cecilia, whose face was downcast. She didn't have her parents or brother to return to once this was all over. Noah felt a pang of sorrow for her.

We've reached that bridge, he thought. *If there's a right moment, this is it.*

He swallowed hard and said, "I hope I don't have to miss you, CeCe."

She gave him a gentle smile. "Like I said before, don't get soft on me now, Teslow. We got all night to talk about the future." Noah sensed she was trying her best to sound comforting, but it fell short.

"Right-O," Nikita said. "Let's get to it."

Nikita placed her helmet on, as did Noah and Cecilia. The room dissolved into its usual wireframe model and then bloomed into photorealistic 3D as the simulation rendered Ottawa's Wellington Street, in front of Parliament Hill. The sky was overcast and Noah felt oddly out of place, standing in front of a building he'd seen so many times on TV. The iconic Peace Tower was situated in the middle of the Centre Block, like a mock-Gothic space rocket.

More like Tyranny Tower, he thought.

The trio walked on a pathway leading to the Peace Tower. In the middle of the walkway stood the Centennial Flame, a monument installed in 1967 to mark Canada's 100 years of Confederation. Noah stood in front of the fountain and studied it; the structure was surrounded by the protective shields of Canada's provinces and territories. He looked toward the center, mesmerized by the dancing LED flame.

"I remember when they replaced the natural gas flame. Back in C5+, which feels like a lifetime ago," Nikita said next to him.

"Why'd they do that?" Cecilia asked.

"The usual reasons," Nikita said and shrugged. "Years of public scrutiny demanding for the change. Our government imposed a carbon tax on citizens before the pandemic, to encourage more eco-friendly options in all sectors of industry, while the government remained hypocritical, as usual, and used natural gas to light the flame twenty-four-seven. On parliament soil."

"I don't see the point to any of this. Who would care that much about a flame?" Noah said.

"It wasn't about the flame, kiddo," she said. "It was about climate change. In fact, many of the world's leaders dedicated more of their efforts to reduce greenhouse emissions by C7+. You two ever hear about the Paris Agreement?"

"No," he said.

"Yes," Cecilia said and stared at the ground. "The agreement was an international treaty, signed in C4– to keep the nations of the world accountable in their fight against climate change."

"I'm impressed, CeCe. Here I was thinking I'd have to give the whole history lesson on my own," Nikita said. "Those in power wanted to curb global warming below two degrees Celsius compared to pre-industrial levels, to achieve a climate neutral world by mid-century. But how could an ordinary person sympathize for the environment when their health and livelihoods were in danger from COVID?"

He heard a whirring in the distance. Behind the Centre Block, a horde of drones rose into the sky above the Library of Parliament. They looked bigger than the usual police drones and instead of black and white detailing, they were striped in red and black.

Nikita's face darkened. "RCDP drones."

"Um, excuse me? What?" Cecilia said.

"Royal Canadian Drone Police," Nikita repeated. "The RCDP replaced the Royal Canadian Mounted Police around the same time as the

Defund the Police movement was happening. Same criticisms, same outcome: the RCMP were replaced by drones. Except these bad boys are ten times more lethal than regular police drones in real life, and I'm sure they'll be more challenging than the usual drones we've faced in here."

"We've never faced these drones before," Noah said. "Did you change the simulation settings?"

"Wasn't me," Cecilia said.

"Me neither," Nikita said. "What's a little more of a challenge for us?"

The RCDP drones swarmed them around the Centennial Flame. Noah raised his bubble shield and huddled into Cecilia and Nikita, who did the same. A barrage of rounds smashed into their shields, sparking as they ricocheted away. The weight of the rounds pressed them further into each other and the noise made Noah's head rattle. He charged his phase-shift gun and shot blindly upwards at a drone. It dodged the blast with magnificent ease. Noah fired a few more times but each shot was easily evaded.

"I can't hit any of them!" he yelled.

"We have to change tactics!" Nikita cried. "Follow my lead. Let's try focusing our aim on one drone. The one at ten o'clock."

Noah aimed at the drone Nikita pointed to.

"On my count," she shouted. "One, two, three!"

They all fired in sync. The drone was unable to move without being struck by one of the beams and it exploded in a flash of fire and sparks. It spun away, launching into the sky as its arsenal of cannon ammunition was detonated by the electrical fire in its motors.

"We got one!" Cecilia cried above the continuing onslaught.

"That was real good, team," Nikita said. "Let's work our way around them all. We have to keep moving. Head east toward Fairmont Chateau Laurier."

They sprinted toward the hotel in a crouch, firing up in unison as they ran. They destroyed each RCDP drone in turn with concentrated blasts. The sky cleared and Noah caught his breath as they reached the hotel's entrance. Just as he was about to relax a little, more red and black drones appeared from around the block. Noah, Cecilia, and Nikita crowded into the lobby and crouched under the big window next to the doors. The drones sailed past without stopping.

"Finally, a break," Nikita sighed.

"We've almost finished the simulation," Noah said. "Let's clear the last of these drones and get out of here."

Nikita and Cecilia nodded.

Outside the hotel, they heard the cry of a familiar voice.

"Help! Help!"

"That sounds like Tommy Chin, doesn't it?" Cecilia breathed. "He must have joined the simulation."

"You're right, kiddo," Nikita said. "But why?"

Noah's eyes narrowed. "This is his first time inside with us."

Looks like he has the guts to come in here after all, he thought.

Tommy came running down the open street beyond the window, his shield and gun inactivated.

"We have to get him," Noah said and stood up. "He's not screwing up our win streak."

Nikita nodded. "Let's go."

They crashed through the hotel doors into the street and sprinted to Tommy, surrounding him with bubble shields raised. A moment later, the RCDP drones reappeared. But there were more of them now.

"I count eleven at nine o'clock and sixteen at three o'clock," Noah shouted.

"CeCe, Noah," Nikita said, "you two take the nine o'clock drones, I got the rest covered." Sweat coated her face and she was breathing heavily. Noah remembered just how much older than him she was. "And *you*," she hissed at Tommy. "Did you bother going through the General's instructional video? Activate your shield and gun now!"

Tommy patted his pockets while the others shot at the drones.

"Nik, we're vulnerable out on the street," Noah said.

"You're right. Let's get some coverage inside the hotel."

They rushed back across the street with their shields up. Cecilia kicked the hotel doors open and they entered one by one. The lobby contained a concrete fountain with two angels at the apex, spouting water, and grand stairways on either side curved gracefully up to the first landing. Golden chandeliers lit the room from high above.

"Up the stairs," Nikita said. "We'll have a better vantage point there. You two go to the right. I'll go left with GI Joe here. We'll go for the old pincer movement." She glanced at Tommy. "And what did I say about activating your gun and shield? Sheesh!"

When Noah was halfway up the stairs, the drones burst through the lobby windows in an explosion of safety glass onto the carpet, immediately opening fire. Noah and Cecilia dropped to a crouch as they scrambled upwards, shields raised, firing over their shoulders. The drones were more powerful than the ordinary police drones, but they seemed more delayed in their sharp movements. Perhaps it was just because they were heavier, weighed down with more armor and greater firepower.

One down, Noah told himself. *Two down, three down, four.*

They reached the first landing and moved toward the center of the railing. Along the landing, Nikita was crouched behind her shield, aiming and shooting deliberately. Tommy was still scrambling to find the orbs in his HAZMAT suit. Two more drones exploded below and spiraled into the fountain, boiling the water in a hiss of steam and vapor.

"Only three to go and then we're out of this hellhole!" Nikita yelled over the cacophony.

Noah kept shooting at the final three drones, but they zig-zagged out of range. Above, the chandeliers were on fire, and paintings around the lobby were in flames. Cecilia had one eye closed, her tongue poking from the corner of her mouth as she tracked a drone. Nikita managed to shoot another drone down just as Tommy finally activated his shield and phase-shift gun.

As Noah edged closer to the center of the balustrade, he heard another drone explode thanks to Cecilia. To his right, Nikita looked determined to get the last one. She focused on her target and took her shot.

Tommy was crouched slightly behind her. He lifted his right arm, which was encased with the gun now, but he struggled to operate its firing capability. In frustration, Tommy swung his arm in a wide arc and struck Nikita's back. Noah registered the situation a moment too late. Cecilia screamed as Nikita toppled over the balustrade into the concrete fountain below.

The room was lit by fire as the last drone erupted in flames.

Noah stared open-mouthed at Tommy.

Tommy met his eyes and whispered, "Oops."

Chapter Thirty

Noah glanced over the balustrade. Nikita was facedown and motionless, and his face-shield's heads-up display didn't register her vital signs, confirming his worst fears. He stopped thinking. He couldn't think. He charged along the landing at Tommy. "You monster!" he roared. "What have you done?"

"It was a mistake," Tommy said and lowered his weapon. "It's my first time using one of these things."

Noah ran straight at Tommy who raised his hands in the air. Once Noah got close enough, he launched himself at Tommy and they rolled across the carpet. Noah pinned Tommy's arms down with his knees and screamed in his face, "She was one of our own! Why'd you kill her?"

Tommy had a look of shock on his face. "It was an accident. I didn't mean her any harm."

"Bullshit," Noah said. "I read your profile. You've always had a thing against authority figures."

"Believe what you want to believe," he said coldly.

Noah raised his bubble shield over Tommy's head. He heard Cecilia behind him, running across the landing.

"Noah, don't!" she shouted. "He'll be dealt with by the General!"

Noah saw her press the emergency response button on the side of her Hover helmet. An alarm suddenly blared.

"You don't have it in you to hurt me," Tommy said. "You're weak."

Noah smashed his shield into Tommy's Hover helmet as hard as he could. The visor cracked down the middle. He pictured Jasmine's face superimposed on Tommy's behind the HAZMAT suit's face-shield and he lifted his bubble shield again. Tommy squirmed under him, his eyes wide. Noah slammed the shield down again, shattering Tommy's face-shield and knocking him out cold.

Cecilia reached his side and stared down at Tommy's bloody face. "Noah . . ."

The hotel pixelated and dematerialized; the chandeliers, paintings, fountain, and flames melted into a wireframe model, which finally vanished to leave only the empty Simulation Chamber. Noah, Tommy, and Cecilia remained on top of the metal stairway in the middle of the room, while Nikita lay below. *SIMULATION COMPLETE* appeared on Noah's visor.

Other FLIGHT members filtered into the Simulation Chamber and a crowd slowly gathered. Noah carefully rose to his feet and turned off his gun and shield. The crowd gathered around Nikita, whispering.

Moments later, the chamber was swamped with people. Eamon and General Vizor were last to join. The room fell silent as General Vizor strode toward Nikita's lifeless body. He stood over her for a minute, his forehead deeply creased. He stared above and Noah caught his stone-black eyes. Vizor climbed up the stairs and wheezed as he peered at Tommy. Noah quivered as he waited for him to say something.

"You killed my best fighter," he murmured. "Then you harmed the one guy who was going to help deliver my message tomorrow."

"General," Noah said, "please listen—"

"You have caused irreparable damage."

"It's not his fault," Cecilia cried.

Vizor shot her a contemptuous look and turned back to Noah.

Eamon ran up to the General. "Bernard, hear them out. There's got to be an explanation for all of this."

"I'm done with explanations," he said, turning on his heel to face Eamon. "I'm going to do what I should've done with your son as soon as he stepped foot in here. He motioned to the cadre of guards standing by the chamber entrance. "Get them out of my sight," he said.

Four armed men in camo-green HAZMAT suits climbed the stairs and grabbed Noah and Cecilia by the arms.

"Throw them into the Crypt!" the General thundered.

Chapter Thirty-One

The guards held Noah tightly and led him down the steps, but he didn't resist. He'd get his chance to explain the events that unfolded and show how Tommy murdered Nikita. Behind him, he could hear Cecilia crying. He should have kept his emotions in check, though his life before had been so cosseted he'd never even suspected his temper could be so ferocious. Even worse was that he'd dragged Cecilia down with him, guilty by association. He couldn't imagine how she must feel at being thrown back into a cage.

Noah watched as his father and a couple of medics tended to Tommy on the landing above. A body bag lay on the floor nearby, unzipped and ready for Nikita. As he was hauled out of the Simulation Chamber, Noah saw contempt on the faces of those he'd come to consider his family. He would inevitably be blamed for destroying The Great

Restart, for single-handedly unraveling decades of hard work and planning.

Goodwill was in the crowd. Noah had rarely seen him without a grin on his face, but now he was somber. He looked at Noah and Cecilia and lowered his head. Beside him, Viktor watched with disgust etched into the creases of his face.

Noah and Cecilia were bustled through the empty hangar, silent apart from the soft hum of computer gear. The guards led them to the Crypt on the eastern side.

Of course, it had to be me, Noah thought. *How am I going to get out of this one?*

One of the guards released Cecilia and grabbed a ring handle in the hangar floor. He grunted as he lifted a round wooden door. He heaved it open and flipped it over onto the floor, raising billowing dust.

"In you go," one of Noah's guards said and pushed him forward. "You too, girl."

Cecilia bumped into Noah and they both stumbled into the hole. Noah grabbed at the lip of the opening to stop himself from tumbling down.

"If I could just talk to General Vizor—" Noah said.

"Shut up and move," the guard said and pushed him down the first step.

He and Cecilia carefully descended the dusty, stone steps. The guard followed them and flicked a switch just inside the opening. Dimly flickering lights danced on the wall and in the space below. A dozen steps led to a dirt floor landing. Along the left-hand wall were four barred jail cells.

"It's about time we got use out of this place, hey, Lockheed?" the tallest guard said. "I was beginning to think we built it for nothing."

"It wasn't for nothing, Smitty," the senior guard, Lockheed said. "It's Vizor's only port in and out of this place. Now, throw them into their cells." He opened one of the cell gates and Noah was shoved in by the others.

"Hey," Smitty said. "They still got their orbs and Hover helmets."

"So, go and grab them, idiot," Lockheed said.

Noah's orbs and helmet were pulled away by the other guards and the cell clanged shut. Lockheed secured the old-fashioned mortice lock with a big key and all the guards headed back up the steps. Noah saw Cecilia through the bars, backing up in her own cell next to his and crouching on the floor.

"This is what happens when you piss off the General," Lockheed said from the foot of the steps and hurried upward. The trapdoor swung shut with a thud and Noah and Cecilia were left alone in the uneasy, unsteady lights of the Crypt.

Noah's cell was about ten by ten square feet. Three of the walls were made of rusty black bars, and the back wall was composed of loose bricks. He crossed to Cecilia's cell and gripped the bars between them. He listened to her tears for a few minutes before speaking.

"CeCe, I'm so sorry I got you into this mess. It's all my fault. I don't know what to say."

Cecilia glanced over at him, her face streaming with tears.

"Please don't say anything, Noah."

Chapter Thirty-Two

They sat in the Crypt for hours, the harsh silence dividing them further than the bars between their cells. Cecilia stopped crying but remained dejected in her dark corner, like a wilted flower. Noah sat alone, brewing his thoughts.

Noah recounted the advice his dad had given him; he was reminded no matter the situation, to be the better man and walk away.

Those disputes never accounted for the death of a friend, he argued with himself.

Still, he couldn't help but wonder if Nikita's death was on him; if he hadn't challenged Tommy to enter the Simulation Chamber, Nikita would still be alive.

I really screwed up this time, he kept repeating to himself. *What is FLIGHT going to do tomorrow? How are they going to get their message across without Tommy? Surely, General Vizor wasn't relying on one person for his whole plan to succeed. Is Tommy even going to be okay?*

Noah figured the General must either be scrambling to find someone else to hijack the government's broadcast, or devising a last-minute contingency plan.

He had no way of knowing what time it was, but he was sure it had to be late evening by now. His eyes were heavy and he wanted to speak with Cecilia before he fell asleep. But she didn't seem inclined to talk to him.

We'll talk in the morning, he told himself. *She needs her space right now.*

He lay on the dirt facing Cecilia's cell, hands under his cheek. He watched her, hoping she would look over at him, but she never moved. Eventually, his eyes got the better of him and he fell into an uneasy sleep.

*

He awoke hours later to find Cecilia standing against the rusted cell bars, watching him. There were barely audible rumblings overhead. Today had to be the day—July 1st, C50+.

"Good morning," she said.

He rose stiffly and walked over to her. "Good morning to you, too. You doing okay?"

"I'm fine," she replied. "I just needed time to myself. What happened up there in the Simulation Chamber . . . it shouldn't have gone that way."

"I know," he said and held Cecilia's hands through the bars. "We'll get out of here. General Vizor can't keep us down here forever."

She nodded serenely but glanced upward suddenly. "You hear that?"

"Hear what?"

"Listen," she hissed and brought her index finger up to her face-shield.

Noah focused his attention but he heard nothing.

And then he heard it.

From above the ceiling, there were screams.

"What the—?"

Something changed in Cecilia then. She pulled away from him and stood in the center of her cell, wringing her hands. "Noah, I need to ask you something," she said, her eyes brimming with tears.

"About?"

"You remember that night we talked about the future? When you asked me what I wanted most in this life?"

"What's that got to do with—?"

"Just listen. If you had a chance to get back what you most wanted in the world . . ." She met his gaze squarely. "Would you do anything for it?"

"CeCe, what are you talking about?"

She took a step toward him. Her eyes, though spilling tears, were fierce and defiant. "If you could find a way to bring your mom back, would you? Would you trade *everything* for her?"

"I don't know what you're talking about. What's gotten into you?"

She lowered her head. "I'm afraid I haven't been all that honest with you. Or with anyone else, for that matter."

The trapdoor above scraped open and thudded to the floor. The sound of gunfire was suddenly unmistakeable. Noah peered through the dimly lit dungeon to make out anything he could see. A pair of black shoes appeared on the top step and began descending. Noah shivered involuntarily. The lights flickered wildly all around.

A pale, bald man in round spectacles reached the bottom of the steps and entered the Crypt. He wore a red leather trench coat. Five red and black RCDP drones hovered on the steps behind him. He strolled toward the cells with his hands clasped behind his back. He stopped in front of Noah's cell. The RCDP drones formed a semi-circle behind him, buzzing like a kicked beehive. He removed his black face mask, revealing his hooked nose and deviant smile.

"Walter Geist?" Noah said, peering into the man's crimson eyes.

The bald man's spectacles gleamed in the flickering light. He spoke with a trace of an accent. "My sweet CeCe," he said. "So very nice to see you again."

Noah turned to Cecilia. "CeCe, what's going on? This man works for OWN—how does he know you?"

Cecilia ignored him and marched to the front of her cell.

"Hello, Mister Ghost."

Chapter Thirty-Three

"Ghost?" Noah said.

"That's right," Geist said without taking his eyes off Cecilia. "I was CeCe's legal guardian for many years. She's been a very valuable asset for OWN Industries. Very valuable indeed."

Noah pressed himself to the bars between their cells and stared at her. "This whole time . . ." he said, though he didn't know if he had enough breath to finish what he wanted to say. "You—you've been working against me? Against FLIGHT? Everything that's happened between us was a lie?"

He felt like he was in some sort of twilight zone; first Jasmine, now CeCe, both spies for OWN Industries?

"Noah" Cecilia cried. "It wasn't like that. It wasn't a lie. Everything I feel for you is real! I was never supposed to get involved with anyone. It was just a happy accident."

"And a happy accident is all it will ever be," Geist said, smirking. The five drones whirred enthusiastically, their cameras and weaponry fixed on Noah and Cecilia.

Noah stared at the dirt floor. He couldn't bare to look at Cecilia any longer.

"Don't be so hard on Miss Flores, young man," Geist said smoothly. "She was simply doing her job."

"He groomed me from the start, Noah," Cecilia said. "He pushed for me to study linguistics, to spend years mastering languages. When he finally felt I was ready, he placed the language-teaching ad in the local newspaper. General Vizor saw the potential in my skills and took the bait. He hired me as one of FLIGHT's communications specialists."

"That's right," Geist said, pacing back and forth. "The Canadian government has been useless in trying to capture the elusive General Vizor. We at OWN Industries took it upon ourselves to infiltrate FLIGHT. I adopted many different orphans over the years, training them to best serve OWN. My brilliant CeCe has been my best investment to date."

"If OWN and the government knew about FLIGHT's plans all along, why did you wait so long to act?"

"FLIGHT has been very useful from a counter-intelligence standpoint," Geist said simply. "We wanted to understand our enemy's reach and see how many traitors existed; how many were ready to expose the truth about COVID. We were never going to let that happen. You're familiar, of course, with the documents your friend Tommy retrieved from the government? They were planted, to catch Vizor's attention. Young Tommy was merely a pawn, but he didn't know it. The documents proved to be quite difficult to decipher, so Vizor sent them to other FLIGHT hubs across the country for help breaking them, something he had never done before, to keep each hub safeguarded. That mistake gave us his whole FLIGHT operation on a silver platter."

"Everything we've been working on . . . it was all for nothing," Noah said hollowly.

Geist nodded. "There is something poetic about crushing one's hopes and dreams at the last second. The broadcast was never going to happen today, young man. FLIGHT was in checkmate long before it made its first move. Thanks to CeCe, OWN was one step ahead of Vizor all along."

"But how were you in contact with Geist this whole time?" Noah asked Cecilia.

She turned away.

The truth struck him like a hammer. "The broadcasts Goodwill aired! You've been feeding FLIGHT's secrets to Geist through the German-language channel!"

"I had no choice!" she said.

"You always have a choice!"

"Yeah? And look at the choices you've made recently, Noah. Not the greatest track record."

Noah and Cecilia glared at each other. Above the ceiling, shouts and screams continued. The RCDP drones around Geist shifted their attention briefly to the gunfire above.

Geist lifted a white-gloved hand. "Now, now, children. This is not the time for silly quarrels. CeCe, I simply wanted to extend my gratitude for your service to OWN Industries. As we speak, FLIGHT is being dismantled across the country. The Great Reset will persist."

"What about our deal?" Cecilia said.

Geist raised his eyebrows. "Deal, my dear?"

"The deal you made with me when I was fourteen. That you would deliver my parents back to me if I went through with your stupid plans." She stalked forward and grabbed the bars of the cell door. "You said they were still alive, that OWN had been holding them captive since their disappearance."

"My sweet CeCe . . . I thought you were smarter than that. How am I to know whether or not they're still alive?" Geist cackled. "But it's time for me to get back upstairs. I must pay Vizor a much overdue visit." He turned around and headed for the steps, his drones in tow.

"Ghost!" Cecilia cried. "You made me a promise!" She banged on the bars repeatedly. "You *promised*!"

Geist stopped at the bottom step and reached inside his trench coat. He turned around with a pistol in his hand.

"I promised *nothing*," he said.

He shot Cecilia squarely in the gut.

Chapter Thirty-Four

Noah screamed and flung himself at the bars dividing their cells. Cecilia sat upright on the dirt floor clutching her abdomen. Blood seeped through her HAZMAT suit, a darker, more ominous red than the suit's cherry blossom fabric.

"Enjoy watching your girlfriend die, young man," Geist said and trotted up the stairs, followed by his drones.

Adrenaline galvanized Noah like a lightning strike. He ran to the cell's back wall and yanked at a loose brick. It slid free easily, showering his hands with dust and fragments of petrified mortar. He gripped the brick tightly, rushed to the front of the cell, and hurled the brick through the bars. The last of Geist's drones was at the top of the steps—Geist and the other four had already ascended through the circular door—and Noah's throw was strong and true. The brick struck the drone's underside, smashing the lens of its camera and tilting the drone hard to the right. It veered away from the wall and spun toward Noah, buzzing like a huge, angry wasp. Noah shrank back and braced himself for an attack.

The drone's cannons extended on each flank. A flash of red light slashed through the rusted bars, which sizzled like hot metal in water. Noah ducked as the drone fired wildly, its aim partially compromised by the loss of one of its cameras. The beams flashed around him, cutting more bars and blasting chunks of brick from the back wall. Noah grabbed a fist-sized piece of debris from the floor and scuttled forward. The drone's remaining cameras squinted at him, as a spider regards a trapped fly.

Noah drew his arm back as three or four bars fell out of the door with a deafening clang. He now had a clear line of sight, and he hurled the brick at the drone. It struck the machine dead-center and smashed the two front sets of rotors. Metal blades broke off, spiraling through the air and shattering the rotors behind them. The drone emitted a continuous stream of fire as it tipped backward, cutting furrows in the Crypt's ceiling. It crashed to the floor on its side, all its instruments damaged but firing still at the wall at the foot of the steps.

Noah stood and levered himself through the gap in the bars. He picked one of them up from the floor, a rusted length of metal three feet long. He crossed to the drone and without hesitation, he raised the bar and smashed it down on the drone's CPU housing. There was a spray of sparks and its cannons fell silent. He watched as the barrels retracted into its body, and smashed it again, just for good measure.

He turned to Cecilia, whose mouth was open in shock. "CeCe!" he called. "Just hold on. I'll get you out of there."

Something exploded above the ceiling, and the rumble of it seemed to shake Noah's insides as much as the foundations of the hangar itself. The ground trembled beneath his feet. Dust sifted down on him.

The drone's erratic assault had damaged Cecilia's cell as well as his own and he grabbed the bars at the front and jerked them apart. Two of them came away grudgingly, creating an opening just wide enough for him to slither through.

"C'mon," he said, kneeling by her side. "Let's get you some help."

She winced as he helped her to her feet. "I don't think I can make it," she said. "I can't climb the steps."

"I'll carry you if I have to," he said impatiently and slung her right arm over his shoulder. "Keep pressure on the wound. Hard."

He maneuvered her through the gap in the bars by lifting her off the floor and twisting his body between the bars. She wasn't heavy, but he felt like she might tear his spine from his back. Once he'd pulled himself out, they hobbled up the steps one by one, Cecilia grunting with every movement. She was leaving a trail of blood, which was dripping from her hands and abdomen. By the time they got to the top, they were both panting and Cecilia's face was ashen; her lips were turning blue. Noah pushed his shoulders against the door above and flipped it open.

He stuck his head through the opening and saw carnage. The hangar was ravaged. Some FLIGHT members were running as RCDP drones gunned them down while others had their shields and guns engaged, firing back in a chaos of energy pulses and flashes. Tables were toppled, computer parts strewn, storage crates smashed open, and fires blazing all around. A huge hole had been blasted in the eastern wall and drones were swarming through.

"Noah, you don't have to do this for me," Cecilia gasped, but despite what she'd done, Noah still loved her. She needed medical attention urgently, but he couldn't imagine how he'd find any in this chaos. "Please," she said, as if reading his thoughts. "Find your father and save yourselves."

"I'm not leaving without you."

"It doesn't look good, Noah."

She was right, but he refused to admit it.

"Find your father," she repeated. "I'm ready to be with mine."

Did Cecilia practice a forbidden religion? He realized he didn't know her at all. Yet he'd connected more with her than anyone he'd ever met.

"Rest now, CeCe," he said and eased her gently against the cellar wall below the lip of the opening.

"I love you, Noah Teslow."

Tears streamed down his face. "I love you too, Cecilia Flores."

Her eyes emptied.

Chapter Thirty-Five

Noah pressed his face-shield against Cecilia's, his hands holding the sides of her head. He closed his eyes and vowed that before the day's end, Walter Geist would be dead.

He used her, he thought. *A means to an end. This whole disaster wasn't on her. It was on men like Geist.*

He climbed out of the Crypt into the mayhem. There were a couple of tables lying on their sides to his right and he sprinted toward them, crouching with his head down. He rolled behind them, but nobody shot at him, so he sucked in a shuddering breath and peered around the edge. A dozen feet away, a FLIGHT member in a turquoise HAZMAT suit lay face-down on the concrete, a charred, gaping hole in his back. Noah closed his eyes and swallowed hard, but he'd seen the shield and phase-shift gun lying beside the man's outstretched hand.

"Okay," he whispered to himself. "Okay, okay. Let's do it." He raised himself into a tightly wound crouch, like a sprinter on the start line. "Let's do it," he muttered. "Let's do it. Let's *do it!*"

He screamed the last two words and shot out from behind the tables. Two drones to his left sensed his movement and spun toward him. One of them fired and Noah jumped forward as the floor exploded behind him. He landed beside the dead man and rolled smoothly, grabbing the shield and gun and twisting at the waist. He came out of the roll on his feet and fired back, hitting the drone squarely on its underside. It jerked upward and erupted in debris.

The second drone angled around to come at him. It dropped a smoke bomb, which filled Noah's vision with opaque eddies and whorls. He focused on the sound of the propellers as the drone buzzed toward him and once it was close enough, he fired into the swirling murk before it had a chance to lock onto him.

He dropped back to his haunches and waved his shield to disperse the smoke. He had to find his dad, though the hangar was in such turmoil it was hard to know where to begin searching. He headed for their workstation.

Above his head, drones flew through rising smoke like bats. This was what Noah had trained for in the Simulation Chamber and he was ready. He jumped over a table as a drone fired a heat-seeking RPG at him. He heard it coming and spun around with his bubble shield raised, deflecting the grenade back at the drone, which erupted in flames.

Noah weaved warily through the debris, listening for incoming drones. He finally stumbled across his workstation. The table was splintered through the middle, and beneath it lay a motionless body dressed in a light grey HAZMAT suit.

"Viktor! No!" Noah cried and ran to Viktor's side. His body was peppered with holes and he gripped his Nobel Prize medal loosely. His grey eyes were lifeless. "Not you too, Viktor."

A drone appeared from nowhere, rushing down at him and firing continuously. Noah fell back and covered himself with his bubble shield as energy pulses ricocheted off it. In a pause between shots, Noah fired around the shield at the drone; the pulse clipped a rotor just enough to send the drone whirling away. It crashed into another approaching drone and they both plummeted to the floor.

"Noah!" a voice cried. "Please, help!"

"Goodwill! Where are you?"

"Over here!" An arm waved at him from behind a pile of shattered crates. Noah crawled over and took shelter with him.

"Are you okay?" Noah asked.

"I'm doing alright, son." Goodwill's short, springy grey-black hair was glistening with sweat. His youthful face was lined and showed his true age. "These drones just came out of nowhere. We were completely caught off guard. The General ordered everyone to take arms, but there wasn't enough time." He shook his head. "So many have died."

"I know," Noah said. "Viktor is dead. And so is CeCe."

Goodwill's dark, translucent eyes widened. "How did this happen?"

"I'll tell you everything once we get out of here. But right now, I need to find my dad. Tell me he's still alive."

Goodwill clenched his jaw. "I can't say for certain, son. Last I saw, he was working in the medical bay."

"Then that's where we're going. Let's go."

"Son, I'm afraid this old man don't got anymore fight in him," Goodwill said. "I didn't get a chance to grab any weapons. And even if I did, I never trained to use them."

"Listen to me. I've already lost two good people today. I'm not losing another."

Goodwill sighed and eventually nodded. "Alright, alright. Let's make our move, then."

They crawled out from behind the crates and headed for the medical bay. Goodwill stayed close behind Noah's shield. They avoided gunfire, beams, and bodies alike, using smoke for cover when they could.

The medical bay was deserted. Computers were unattended, beeping for attention. Medical personnel were littered on the floor like discarded disposable masks. None of the bodies wore a white HAZMAT suit with light blue lining.

He might still be alive.

Goodwill grabbed a metal orb from a dead woman in a pale blue suit and when he stood back up, he stared through the glass wall of the fourth observation unit. Noah joined him and looked in at Tommy Chin. He lay immobile in his bed, deep in a coma without his HAZMAT suit on, connected to wires and IVs, his face unrecognizable from the bruising and swelling.

"We can't leave him here to die," Noah said. "We have to help him."

Goodwill nodded. They went single file through the Disinfectant Chamber.

In the observation unit, Noah disconnected the medical equipment from Tommy's body. As he pulled a cannula from Tommy's arm, he glimpsed movement from the corner of his eye. He turned his head slowly and saw a drone beyond the glass wall. It hovered like a patient predator.

"Don't move," Noah said. "It hasn't spotted us yet."

"The reflection from the glass mirror must be obscuring its view. We have to get out of here immediately," Goodwill breathed, seemingly unable to bring himself to look at the drone. "There's oxygen tanks all over the room."

Noah saw five cylinders around the bed. He fumbled the rest of the wires from Tommy. The drone was turning lazily outside, looking for targets. When it turned away, Noah raised his gun and fired through the window, five quick blasts one after the other. The glass shattered into gummy fragments immediately, but every shot missed the drone. It whirled around to face them.

"Shit," Noah said, lowering his gun.

"We have to ditch him," Goodwill said. "Or we're all going down." He activated his shield and hunched behind it.

The drone opened fire. With shields raised, Noah and Goodwill leaped through the broken window, landing directly under the drone. An energy pulse penetrated one of the oxygen tanks, which exploded like a grenade. The blast thrusted them ten feet into the medical bay and hurled the drone into the wall behind it. Its rotors snapped off and its lights went out. In the observation unit, flames engulfed Tommy's inert form.

"Are you hurt?" Noah asked.

"I should be asking you the same thing," Goodwill replied as Noah pulled him to his feet. Noah shook his head. "Looks like we're both still standing, then."

They peered back at Tommy, whose body was charred to an unrecognizable crisp. Noah lowered his head and out of the corner of his eye, he witnessed Goodwill make the Sign of the Cross.

They headed back out of the medical bay and Noah cautiously examined the hangar. The screams and shouts had died down but at the far end of the north wall, he saw two men surrounded by drones. One wore a navy-blue HAZMAT suit, and the other a white HAZMAT suit with light blue lining.

"Dad!" he cried and bolted out into the hangar. Goodwill uttered a couple of choice expletives and followed.

Noah was out of breath by the time he reached them, but they'd managed to take out the drones without any help from Noah. The General clapped Eamon on the shoulder as the last drone fell and they both turned to see Noah approach.

Eamon's eyes widened dramatically. "*Noah*! You're okay!"

"I'm alive and well too, doc," Goodwill called, some way behind. "Thanks for checking."

Eamon ran to his son and hugged him tightly. "I thought I'd lost you," he said. "The General didn't allow anyone into the Crypt. Once the drones attacked us, my first instinct was to come and find you." He glanced at the debris all around them. "We . . . ah, got held up."

"Dad, you don't have to explain yourself. I understand. No one could have predicted this."

"No one but your little girlfriend," General Vizor spat. "Isn't that right?"

"She was manipulated by OWN," Noah said defiantly.

"Forget it," Vizor said. "We can discuss it when we're in a more secure location. At the onset of this ambush, I activated my emergency response team. They should be here by now."

"What about the rest of the FLIGHT crew?" Noah said.

Vizor swept his arm around. "Look around you, kid. There isn't anyone else standing. It's just the four of us left."

Noah heard the noise of loud engines coming from outside.

"Come on," Vizor said and gripped Noah's shoulder. "The birds are waiting."

Chapter Thirty-Six

There were no exit doors in the corner of the north wall, so Noah, Eamon, and General Vizor charged up their guns and fired at the wall in front of them, concentrating their energy blasts until a wide circle of the corrugated metal surface began to glow red. Within a few minutes, the edges of the circle started to melt, and it finally detached itself from the rest of the structure and fell outwards onto the grass outside, setting fire to it. Goodwill, who still only had a shield, stood well back. The hangar ceiling creaked and one by one, they carefully stepped out through the smoldering hole.

The sudden sunlight was blinding and Noah had to cover his eyes. When he could finally open them again, he saw nothing but thick, wavy grass and blue sky streaked with high clouds. Finally, he saw a concrete path in the grass, cracked and overgrown, that led to a runway; twelve pale blue Learjets were lined up in single-file on it.

"Bombardier Learjet 75 Liberties," Vizor said proudly to Noah. "Acquired them years ago. I have pilots on standby for an emergency like this. Unfortunately, I didn't think there'd be so few survivors. We'll only need one jet." He pointed to the lead plane, which looked unbelievably huge and powerful to Noah.

Noah had never imagined he would ever see—let alone ride in—an aircraft. He remembered Grandpa John's stories about a world where planes filled the skies, carrying passengers to every corner of the Earth. Noah suddenly wished his grandparents were here with him, to share this moment.

"What's the plan?" Noah said, turning to Vizor.

"I'm curious about that myself," Eamon said.

"Yeah," Goodwill said, peering around the airfield nervously. "Where will we go?"

Vizor sighed. His broad shoulders fell. "We're going to a safe house in Montreal. I have a contact there who's agreed to take us in until we figure out what to do. That's as far as I've got."

To Noah, Vizor was no longer an authoritarian general, a bluff commander of men, but simply a tired old man—and his grandfather. Vizor had dedicated his life to his cause, for truth and justice. Everyone at FLIGHT had believed in him and his ideals. And now, it was all gone. Life would remain the same, for Noah and the rest of the world. The masses would continue to be manipulated by the elite.

On the runway, the lead jet's side door slowly opened, flipping down to reveal a set of steps up to the fuselage.

"We better get going," Eamon said. "There are probably more drones on the way."

Vizor led them down the path to the runway, with Noah at the back. The sun gleamed on the aircraft's wings and body. The sound of idling jet engines was deafening.

They stepped onto the concrete of the runway. Vizor and Eamon reached the steps when someone suddenly grabbed Noah from behind. He felt a forearm around his throat, choking him, and a pistol against his temple. He glimpsed, from the corner of his eye, a white-gloved hand.

The other three men turned around and Eamon gasped. Four RCDP drones buzzed into Noah's line of sight, their artillery pointed at the group.

"Geist," Eamon said quietly, "let go of my son." He raised his gun and shield; Vizor did the same.

"Not another move or I blow his brains out," Geist said.

The drones closed in and Noah heard Geist's breathing, heavy in his ear. The men froze at the foot of the steps, even Goodwill, who'd barely moved.

"There we go," Geist said. "All I ask is a little cooperation." He pressed the gun's muzzle harder against Noah's head. "Now, deactivate your weapons and toss the orbs onto the grass. *Now*."

They did as they were told.

"What do you want?" Goodwill asked. "The boy means you no harm."

"It's me he wants," Vizor said.

Geist smirked. "That I do. You've been on the run a long time. So good to see you again, old friend."

"The feeling isn't mutual," Vizor said. He looked like a ferocious dog held at bay on a chain. "Leave my grandson alone. If it's me you want, it's me you've got."

"Oh, he's your grandson, is he? How very interesting. Prime Minister Talbot is going to be so pleased to have you back in the capital. I can only imagine what the government will do to you for abandoning your post . . . and our cause. It's a shame, because you had so much potential. And you threw it all away, for nothing."

"For everything!" Vizor barked. "What the G7 did was unforgivable. I blame myself every day for having any part in it. FLIGHT was my opportunity to right my wrongs. To give the world another chance."

"As I've already explained to your dear grandson, you never had a chance," Geist said and laughed. "We own you. I ought to teach you a lesson, to show you what happens when a coward runs away from his duty."

Vizor raised his arms, the posture of a man surrendering unconditionally. "He's innocent, Geist. He doesn't deserve this."

"Don't tell me what is and isn't deserved! I lost my wife and my unborn child due to the likes of you. As far as I'm concerned, FLIGHT is nothing more than a fancy name for an anti-mask rally. An excuse for those who don't care to follow orders, who consider themselves above the safety of others."

"If that's what you think, then you're a fool," Vizor said. "We've developed a vaccine to get us out of this mess. You could be a part of it."

"We don't need a vaccine. We have my Distance Bands. Plus, I've gotten quite used to the order of things. There's no turning back now."

The pistol trembled against Noah's head. He closed his eyes tightly.

Everyone held their breath.

Five shots were fired.

Noah didn't know what death felt like, but he was quite certain it wasn't this. He opened his eyes and saw his father, grandfather, and Goodwill rushing toward him. The arm was gone from around his throat, the gun from his head.

A black metallic sphere the size of a tennis ball hovered at the top of the jet's steps with its propulsion-backing system. It slipped smoothly back into the aircraft and Noah twisted around. Walter Geist lay on his back, one leg convulsing spasmodically. His jaw worked silently for a moment and then his body went rigid. One lens of his spectacles was cracked and there was a small, neat hole in the center of his forehead. His crimson eyes were wide open. Noah glanced away from the mess spread out on the concrete beyond Geist and saw that the four drones had also been taken down. They lay on the runway as lifeless as Geist.

Eamon reached Noah and hugged him fiercely. Goodwill and even Vizor joined in. They all stared inside the jet's doorway, and whoever—or whatever—might be there.

"Whatever that sphere was, it clearly didn't want us dead," Vizor said. He moved toward the steps. "Let's take a look but keep your guard up."

"Stay close to me from now on," Eamon said. "I don't want you out of my sight again." He led Noah up the steps behind Vizor. Goodwill brought up the rear.

The interior of the cabin was carpeted in cherry red, with beige leather seats and oakwood counter railings below the windows. Noah walked down the aisle, which was illuminated by LED lighting. There was no sign of the hovering sphere.

"Welcome aboard, gentlemen," a female voice said over the intercom. "Please take a seat and make yourselves comfortable."

"The pilot?" Noah said.

Vizor nodded. "Must be. Nobody else has access to these planes."

"What about that mini-Death Star?"

"I don't know," he said, checking around the cabin for any signs of suspicion.

Noah sat in a chair, too exhausted to do anything else. They were here now; there was nothing more he could do. His father eventually sat uneasily opposite him, while Goodwill and Vizor sat next to them across the aisle. Noah let himself sink into the cushioned chair.

The jet moved forward, lined itself up on the runway, and slowly picked up speed. Noah looked out the window and his heart started racing immediately, at the sight of the ground rushing past so quickly. The front of the jet rose and Noah felt as if he might tumble from his seat. And just like that, they were airborne and swinging right, the plane's wing dipping steeply. As they climbed, Noah saw the hangar below. The ceiling had collapsed and flames were dancing and reaching through the hole.

The plane eventually leveled off and raced above the ground. The cockpit door opened and a figure emerged, dressed in a black HAZMAT suit. It leaned on an empty chair at the front and removed its tinted face-shield. Noah watched jet-black hair fall free and saw an olive-skinned face, mutilated by scars. Her hazel eyes glanced over Noah and found Eamon.

"Hello again, husband," Jasmine said.

Chapter Thirty-Seven

"Jasmine," Eamon gasped. "You—You're alive."

"You sound so disappointed," she said. "What can I say? I'm a survivor."

"But how? I was certain you were dead."

Jasmine's irritation surfaced beneath her scars. "My Distance Band's distress signal activated after the crash. A medi-drone flew me to the nearest hospital. I was in an ICU bed for months. It took countless surgeries and endless hours of rehabilitation to get to where I am today."

Vizor attempted to get up from his seat.

"Not so fast," Jasmine said and pulled the black sphere from a pocket of her suit, moving without any indication of disability. She tossed it into the air, where it hovered above her head. Red lights lit up along the cube's edges and Noah saw red spots appear on his chest—and the chests of the rest of the group. "Sit back down, old man," Jasmine snapped. "This little gadget is courtesy of OWN Industries. It's a Tracker, one of Geist's own designs. You make any sudden movements and it'll kill you. There's another one in the cockpit, directed at the pilot."

The General slowly sank back into his seat.

"That's a good boy," she taunted.

"Where are you taking us?" Eamon asked.

"Same place Geist was taking you. To the capital. The Prime Minister is expecting you for the C50+ celebrations today and I'm here to deliver him the dessert."

"Why'd you kill Geist?" Vizor said. "You both serve the same devil, don't you?"

"Geist demoted me for my mishap on Highway Seven," Jasmine said, her voice entirely devoid of emotion. "Despite my years of loyalty, he sold me out. He had no sympathy for an agent who failed her mission. I needed to find a way to prove my worth again, to OWN and to the G7. That meant delivering you, General, back to the government myself. I couldn't let Geist take the credit. That old fool had his time. I saw my opportunity and took my shot. Literally."

"But how did you know where to find us?" Noah asked.

Jasmine answered him, but looked at Eamon as she spoke. "I planned carefully, and I got myself on the mission roster. I knew the General would activate his emergency response system once the ambush took place, so I waited for the jets to arrive on the runway. If Vizor escaped the wreckage inside FLIGHT, I knew he would take the lead jet.

You might call it a lucky guess—I call it a man with an ego. Of course, if he'd chosen any other jet, he would've found each pilot dead in it, forcing him to take the lead jet."

"We're all very impressed with your work," Vizor said and looked away, staring disinterestedly out the window. "Great job, detective."

Jasmine stalked down the aisle, the Tracker following her movements, and punched Vizor in the face, hard. "Keep this up and you might not get to meet the Prime Minister after all."

Vizor looked up at her levelly, blood pouring from his nose and cut lip.

Noah looked away. Beyond the window, high in the bright blue sky, there was no way out but down.

"Make your peace now, gentlemen," Jasmine said. "We'll be in Ottawa soon. Enjoy the last few hours of your miserable lives."

Chapter Thirty-Eight

The rest of the flight was uneventful. Eamon was lost in thought as he gazed out the window, concern etched into his face. Noah could only imagine what he must be thinking, but he was sure it must be full of loss and regret.

Eventually, the jet slowed and tipped forward as it began its descent, which caused Noah's stomach to churn. Blinding sunlight streamed through the window as the plane tilted toward a tiny ribbon of runway thousands of feet below.

Jasmine stood up from her seat at the front of the cabin, tossing a magazine aside. The scars on her face had become angry red weals in the dry, pressurized atmosphere. "Once we arrive in Ottawa, OWN agents will assist you into a designated vehicle," she said. "You'll be transported to Parliament Hill, where you'll take part in the festivities."

"Jasmine," Eamon said. "You don't have to do this."

"Yes, I do," she said.

He shook his head. "You could be free from all of this. You don't have to serve OWN anymore. General Vizor can make things right. He can deliver a life where nobody needs to worry about COVID-37 or any other variant, ever again. We'll have our freedom back."

"OWN has already provided me with freedoms the rest of you don't have," Jasmine said dismissively. "Do you see me wearing a HAZMAT helmet? A mask? OWN agents are already vaccinated and protected. I can breathe the open air without succumbing to COVID-37, unlike the rest of you. Once you're delivered to Talbot, I'll gain privileges the likes of which you could only dream of." She glared at them defiantly, but Noah saw deep sadness in her eyes.

"You don't even believe what you're saying," Noah said. "You're not free. You'll never be free."

"I spent two agonizing years with you and your whining dad," she spat, "creating a façade of a family. I've sacrificed many years to OWN and I'll sacrifice a hundred more if I must. I'm not going back to the streets."

The jet's wheels suddenly squealed on the runway, jolting the cabin and making them all gasp. The jet slowed to a halt; Noah was thrust forward in his seat, gripping his arm rests to steady himself.

"Everyone up," Jasmine said as the jet crawled to its drop-off point.

They all stood. The Tracker's lasers followed every move. Jasmine held up her right wrist and pressed something on a bracelet. Noah's face-shield turned black instantly, completely obscuring his vision. He heard cries of confusion from the others.

"I forgot to mention," Jasmine said. "You'll be transported blindly to the party, in case anybody gets any funny ideas about outrunning the Tracker. Which you couldn't anyhow." Noah heard her laugh. "Remember, no sudden movements. The Tracker is focused on you the whole time. You don't want to die before the grand finale, do you?"

Noah heard the aircraft's door swing open and people rushing in. Someone grabbed Noah firmly by the arm and led him down the aisle. Noah walked slowly, heeding Jasmine's warning, but his captor kept pushing him forward. He was bundled through the open door and heard the jet's engines winding down. He gripped the handrails alongside the steps with both hands until he reached the asphalt. None of the others uttered a sound, so he kept quiet too.

A car door opened in front of him and he heard his father grunt as he was forced into the vehicle. Noah's captor pressed his head down and pushed him onto a leather seat across someone's legs. He wriggled upright into a sitting position, shoulder to shoulder with the legs' owner. He heard OWN agents in the car talking quietly amongst themselves. He couldn't tell how many there were, but the car felt big, like a limousine.

The car door eventually slammed shut and Jasmine said to the agents, "Listen up. It's half-past one. We have a fifteen-minute drive to

Confederation Park. The C50+ parade will be starting shortly, so we should be able to catch it and show off our little friends. Make sure you're ready. I'm looking at you, Arsenault."

Arsenault—whoever he was—was the owner of the legs Noah had sprawled across and was now sitting with his wide, hard shoulders pressed into Noah's. Noah heard the agent gulp. "Yes, ma'am."

An agent opposite said, "Forgive me for asking, but where's Mister Geist? We were expecting him at the airport with Vizor and company. No one has been able to reach him."

"He was killed in the line of duty," Jasmine said.

"But he had a troop of security drones—"

"Laurent, do I have to report you for insubordination?" Jasmine said and silence fell. The only sound was the quiet hum of the big car's tires on the road. The tension was palpable, like heat rising in an oven.

"Any further questions?" Jasmine said.

No one said a word the rest of the way.

The vehicle eventually came to a stop and Jasmine said, "Everyone out."

Noah was hauled through the door by, he presumed, Arsenault. He felt grass under his feet. His face-shield cleared suddenly, and Noah saw he was in a deserted tree-filled park. Birds chirped on a glittering fountain in the distance. He finally realized he was in Confederation Park, downtown Ottawa. And from a few feet ahead, the Tracker's laser lit three red spots in the center of his chest.

"The parade is on its way," Jasmine said. "Get the prisoners ready."

Noah got a good look at Arsenault before he was turned around to face the road. Arsenault was a short, stocky man with an upturned nose, and Noah figured he'd been a guy ordered around his entire life.

The historic Lord Elgin Hotel was on the other side of the street, a twelve-story limestone edifice capped by a copper roof. The black limousine that had brought them here drove silently away. Further down the street, a parade of floats was headed their way. Trumpets boomed, fireworks burst in the air, and the Canadian national anthem blared from distorting speakers. The sky was full of red and black RCDP drones, buzzing around the floats and relaying images from their cameras to broadcasters across the globe. Noah squinted as a burst of fireworks formed the shapes of maple leaves and a message that read, *HAPPY C50+, CANADA!*

The first float reached them and glided silently by. The platform was topped with a thirty-foot holographic RCMP officer, dressed in the unmistakable Red Serge uniform and Stetson. He wore a surgical mask and waved a gloved hand at the cameras. The second float bore another hologram, this one a healthcare worker in a white lab coat with a stethoscope around her neck. She washed her hands with soap over a sink then stood, winked, and held up a sheet of paper, the glowing type of which read:

Remember to do your part:

Wash your hands,

Wear your mask,

Keep six feet apart.

We will get through this!

Noah felt sick; the propaganda was too much. Now that he knew the truth about COVID, it was hard to imagine anyone believing the government's lies.

Several other floats passed them as the trumpets continued to shriek, all bearing huge holograms of favored professions, including vaccine scientists and journalists. Another float commemorated Canada's indigenous cultures, the people of the First Nations, with two holographic dancers brilliantly adorned with multi-colored feathers and masks, spinning and whirling to the beat of a tribal drum. Then, a float with the holographic image of a young Prime Minister sailed past. He was dressed in boxing gloves and shorts, using a magnified COVID-37 particle as a punching bag.

The final float stopped in front of Noah and his fellow captives.

"Up you go," Jasmine said and nudged him between the shoulder blades.

Noah stepped toward the float, which lowered to the curb. The Tracker moved ahead, its laser targeting beam pointed at his chest. He climbed the half-dozen steps and Arsenault directed him to the front of the platform. Eamon, Vizor, and Goodwill were pushed into place beside him. Eamon glanced over at his son, his face downcast.

The float moved smoothly off down Elgin Street. Behind them, in the center of the float's platform, a new hologram glowed brilliantly into life: a thirty-foot guillotine with a gleaming, razor-sharp virtual blade quivering atop.

This is the government's statement to the public, Noah thought. *Obey us or die.*

Drone's swarmed around the float as it took a left turn down Albert Street. From somewhere ahead, a female news reporter's voice rang out. "And now we have our final float of this remarkable C50+ parade. Welcome our trusted OWN agents, who continue to serve and protect our country. Up front are four captured terrorists belonging to the rebel organization, FLIGHT."

The lies, Noah thought bitterly.

"Folks at home may remember the father and son duo who murdered their elders inside a long-term care facility before making their escape. They were discovered to be working within FLIGHT with long-time fugitive and disgraced former general, Bernard Vizor. It's been confirmed that the three are blood relations. The black male has yet to be identified but is known to be a part of the terrorist organization as well."

There was a chorus of jeers from speakers along the street. Noah stared at them, his mouth open. The calls came from viewers at home tuned into the program.

"Terrorists!" they cried. "Murderers! Traitors!"

The float took a right turn onto Kent Street.

"What do we do to those who risk the safety of our country?" the reporter called, as if this were some kind of religious litany.

"Kill them!" the crowd bellowed.

"That's right. Our fierce Prime Minister will deal with these traitors promptly, as always."

Noah's heart was pounding through his ribs. He felt clammy and lightheaded. The drones swarmed around his face, the death chants from the faceless crowd reverberated inside his skull, the blaring trumpets and roaring national anthem deafened him. He sucked in a deep, ragged breath and looked desperately at his dad, but Eamon appeared no less panicked. Only Jasmine seemed composed, her scarred face smiling in sick delight.

The float made its final turn onto Wellington Street, stopping in front of Parliament Hill.

"Burn them!" the virtual crowd screamed. "Hang them!"

The final fireworks burst in the sky.

A sharp slice cut through the air.

Noah turned around.

The virtual blade of the guillotine came plunging down.

Chapter Thirty-Nine

The guillotine blade reached its nadir and pixelated into a million pieces, disappearing in the wind. The cacophony of the parade quieted. The sky clouded over.

To Noah's left, the Centennial Flame blazed virtually in front of the Centre Block. The Fairmont Chateau Laurier hotel was straight ahead, exactly the same as its counterpart in the Simulation Chamber. A shiver ran through his body.

"This is our stop," Jasmine said. "Let's go."

The captives were frog-marched down the steps and Noah took his first step onto the curb when the world went black.

Not again, he thought. It was bad enough being monitored by the Tracker, but stumbling around blindly was even worse.

"Jasmine," Eamon said, "we've been cooperative. Please, remove the blinders."

"I don't bargain with terrorists," she said and fell silent.

As Noah crept forward, Arsenault whispered into his ear, "If you weren't ordered to meet the Prime Minister, I'd happily trip you and let the Tracker kill you here on the spot."

Noah ignored him. He felt a sprinkling of rain on the top of his head, and then suddenly it was pouring down, as if someone had emptied a bucket over him. He trudged through the rain as it pattered off his HAZMAT suit. Arsenault led him up another flight of steps and then they were under the cover of a roof. He pictured Parliament Hill and realized they must be at the entrance to the Peace Tower. Doors creaked open in front of him, their sound ringing off the walls of the Centre Block.

As they stepped into the rotunda, the doors clanged shut behind them. There was a stillness in the air; Noah sensed the OWN agents were tense too.

"Follow me," Jasmine said. "The public is excluded from in here; there'll be no more live broadcasts on TV. Whatever happens in these halls is private."

They turned left into a hallway. Their footsteps echoed on marble. The blinder effect disappeared and Noah found himself in the House of Commons foyer. Thick square pillars of black marble stood like great sentinels. Hallways and chambers led off in every direction. The foyer was illuminated by LED torches on the walls; if it weren't for the lights, Jasmine and the OWN agents would have seamlessly camouflaged into the blackness.

Noah gazed up at the ceiling, which was painted admiral blue and resembled a midnight sky. The doors behind the group slid open and Jasmine led them into the House of Commons chamber.

The chamber had been revamped; the green carpet and oak chairs had been replaced with a crimson red carpet and sleek black metal benches. Each was six feet from its neighbor with screens embedded into the desktops. The stained-glass windows had been replaced with Renaissance-style paintings of former Prime Ministers, all of them glaring at Noah and his companions. At the far end of the chamber, a large screen was mounted on the wall, displaying a map of the Canadian provinces with red dots scattered across the country. A dozen RCDP drones hovered above.

This room, once a home of democracy, was now the seat of a totalitarian regime.

Below the large screen, seven figures stood around a circular, black granite table. Six of them were crystal-clear holograms. All were dressed in dark suits; all were staring gravely at the FLIGHT captives. The man with his back to the room was the only one physically present.

"At last, our distinguished guests have arrived," he said in a husky voice. The figure turned around, his grey curly hair swaying. "Jasmine, bring them to me."

"Yes, Mister Prime Minister, sir," Jasmine said. She walked toward him, her Tracker following. The captives were dragged and pushed toward the G7 leaders around the table.

"Please turn off the Tracker, would you?" Talbot said. "These prisoners won't be going anywhere."

The three red dots on Noah's chest finally disappeared. He sighed softly, as did his father, Goodwill, and General Vizor. They were hustled into a line facing the Prime Minister.

"Agents, get our guests some chairs. We don't want to appear inconsiderate, do we?"

Arsenault slid a sleek black metal chair behind Noah's knees, forcing him to sit. As soon as he did, his wrists and ankles were immediately bound against the arms and legs of the chair by Distance Bands attached to the metal. The sight of them made Noah's stomach flip. He'd been foolish to think he could ever escape government control.

Prime Minister Talbot stood before them as his G7 counterparts diffused their soft blue light and looked on with impassive virtual eyes.

Noah met the Prime Minister's all-too-present steel-grey eyes, which burned with rage.

"Please, make yourselves comfortable," Talbot said and shot a reptilian smile.

The RCDP drones swarmed down and encircled the group, cameras sharply focused, artillery at the ready.

"We have so much to discuss."

Chapter Forty

Noah's heart was pounding so fast he thought he might die of a heart attack there and then. He jerked his arms against the cold metal bands of the chair, but it was futile. Goodwill sat to his left, his father to his right, and General Vizor on Eamon's right. Jasmine and the OWN agents stood behind them, alert and poised.

Noah couldn't look away from Talbot's steel-grey eyes; the more he stared into them, the further down the abyss he fell. Growing up, Noah had watched this man speak almost every night after the evening news, but at this moment it was as if he saw Prime Minister Talbot for the first time.

"I have one hour before I must deliver my grand speech to the nation for our C50+ celebration," Talbot said in his resonant, measured tones. "Plenty of time to do away with you all."

"Gregoire," said one of the suited holograms behind him, "perhaps it's best for us to let you handle this matter in private. We trust you will dispose of these terrorists promptly. We can't risk them sabotaging any more of our work. We've come too far."

"No need to worry, Mister President. Please, you have your own C50+ celebrations to prepare for in just three days. Consider this matter handled."

"Very well. If you need anything, the G7 is here."

The six holographic figures walked back to the circular, black granite table. They stood at their stations and saluted Prime Minister Talbot before pixelating then fading away completely. He saluted them back.

"Vizor," Talbot said and strolled around his chair. Two drones hovered behind his shoulders. "You've been on the run for so long. Some presumed you dead, but I heard whispers that you were still active and still calling yourself 'General'. You, the traitor who abandoned his country, his cause, and was stripped of his rank. How do you sleep at night?"

"I should be asking you the same thing," Vizor said. His face was swollen and bruised where Jasmine had punched him.

Talbot closed his eyes and smiled. "Tell me, how does it feel to know that everything you put into FLIGHT was all for . . . nothing? Your personal greed and selfishness lured innocent men, women, and even children to their deaths today."

"Don't you dare put the blame on me!" Vizor shouted. "Every single death is on your head, like the millions of others who've perished from COVID-37. We fought for our rights and freedoms."

"Hm. But where have your rights and freedoms gotten you? Bound to a chair with nowhere to run, nowhere to hide. Thanks to some well-recruited spies, you were never a threat. We had your whole operation from Vancouver to Halifax mapped out from start to finish, waiting for the perfect time to dismantle you. Take a look at the screen."

Noah studied the map. The red dots must've indicated FLIGHT networks, and there was one in almost every province and territory in Canada. He hadn't realized how vast Vizor's operation was.

Vizor hung his head. "I couldn't live with myself serving the tyrants who created lockdown measures and Distance Band enforcements, all based on their own man-made virus. I had to find a way to make things right after The Great Reset. If it was all for nothing, then at least I'll die in peace, knowing I tried."

Talbot kneeled in front of Vizor and lifted his face-shield. He peered into his eyes. "Oh, Bernard, I'm not going to give you the pleasure of a quick and easy death. No, you'll watch your family die first, and then you'll be tortured and imprisoned for the rest of your pathetic life."

He stood abruptly and kicked Vizor in the chest, toppling the chair over backward with Vizor still attached to it.

Jasmine stepped forward as Vizor groaned on the floor. "Mister Prime Minister, sir," she said. "I'd take great satisfaction in dealing with this one personally." She nodded at Eamon.

"Jasmine, you have been an integral part of this special day," Talbot said. "I have always considered OWN as the government's little brother. But do explain to me—how is it that a simple field agent like yourself is standing before me instructing your fellow agents? What happened to my associate, Mister Geist?"

"He was killed in the line of duty, sir. Killed by this boy here." She pointed at Noah.

Talbot glanced at Noah then turned back to Jasmine. "Bullshit," he said. "Mister Geist communicated with me only moments before his death, informing me that the Calgary FLIGHT network had been neutralized. He told me he would bring Vizor to me personally." His cold eyes bore into Jasmine's. "You seized your opportunity to purge of him, didn't you?"

"Sir, please . . ."

"You OWN agents are all the same. Ambitious to the point of recklessness, constantly striving for riches and glory. When did the privilege of receiving our COVID-37 vaccine become insufficient reward? When did serving our cause for the greater good become not enough?"

"Sir, I—"

"You what? You lied to me? Yes. Yes, you did. And you know what we do to liars, don't you?"

Jasmine reached for something at her waist and when she pulled her hand up, Noah saw she grasped her Tracker. She tossed it into the air and the sphere sprung to life, aiming its red lasers at Talbot's chest. Just before it fired, an RCDP drone flew directly into it, spinning it through 180 degrees and its burst of energy struck Jasmine in the neck. She immediately collapsed as blood and smoke sprang from the wound and her open mouth. She writhed for a moment until the gouging blood slowed to a weak pulse and then stopped. Her body became still.

The rest of the OWN agents stumbled backward.

"Wait," Arsenault said. "We didn't—"

Talbot raised his arms and a dozen drones opened fire on the black-suited agents.

Noah didn't turn to look, but he heard bodies thud to the floor.

The drones regrouped around the captives.

Fury ignited in the Prime Minister's eyes.

Blood seeped across the carpet around Noah's feet.

Chapter Forty-One

Talbot stretched expansively, as if waking up after a refreshing nap. "Well then," he said. "Now that we're finally rid of distractions, we can speak without further interruption." He smiled. "This must be the infamous Eamon Teslow. Geist told me all about you and your innovative technology. It's a shame you double-crossed us. I had high hopes for your idea."

Noah saw his father stiffen in his chair. "I don't work with criminals," Eamon said.

The Prime Minister sneered. "The heroes are always the quickest to judge. You're no different than we are, good doctor."

"There's no comparison between you and I."

"None at all?" Talbot stooped to Vizor and pulled his chair roughly upright. The General grimaced but said nothing. "What about the plan you and your dear parents concocted? The one at Villa Salud?"

"It was their wish, not mine."

"You're not free from guilt. You know what you did was criminal. You murdered your own parents." Eamon slumped on his chair. "Your medical license doesn't give you authority to carry out medical assistance in dying, let alone use an illegally-obtained injection of COVID-37 serum."

"My parents wanted it, for the greater good," Eamon said.

"And the hundreds of other End-Generationers inside the long-term care facility? Did they want it too?" Talbot strode along the line and stood in front of Eamon, glaring. "Regardless of your intentions, you killed not only your own parents, but also the rest of the residents in what they'd hoped was a safe haven."

Noah's breath caught in his throat. Everything had happened so quickly in Villa Salud that he hadn't realized until now that when Eamon broke his grandparents' glass pod wall, he'd released the COVID-37 virus into the tunnels and pods of the whole facility.

Talbot smiled at Noah. "That's right, boy," he said. "Your father is no saint. Given their immunocompromised states, the End-Generationers of Villa Salud didn't survive the sudden outbreak he unleashed upon them. For all their talk of enhanced safety protocols, no long-term care facility is immune to our lethal virus. Of course, the news media didn't publicize the event—we didn't want to cause even more panic. Two fugitives on the run for the murder of their family was all anyone needed to hear."

"You've proved your point," Eamon said flatly. To Noah, he looked deflated, hollow. "What do you want from us?"

"I want each of you to understand, good doctor. I want you to understand *why* we do what we do. I want you to understand everything before I kill you."

"There's nothing left to explain," Goodwill said, the first time he'd spoken since they'd gotten here. "We already know COVID-19 was man-made, developed by the G7 decades ago, to demonize China."

Talbot raised his eyebrows. "You've got it all figured out, haven't you?"

"You and your cronies continue to do the work of your predecessors, to manipulate the masses with fear, to make us prisoners of our own homes. And all for what? So the elitists can enjoy privileges the rest of us can't?" There was something in Goodwill's tone, something different about him that Noah couldn't quite pin down.

Talbot laughed. "You act like this is the first time the rich and powerful have manipulated the masses. We're not just wicked and evil, you know. Sometimes, we need to do what others wouldn't dare, to push the world forward. Look at the pharaohs of ancient Egypt; if it wasn't for the enslavement of the Egyptian people, we would never have had the great pyramids."

Noah spoke before he even realized he had anything to say. "And what is it that Canada and the G7 hope to create by enslaving the world?"

Talbot leaned forward so his face was only inches from Noah's face-shield. "It's not what we hope to create, *boy*. It's what we hope to sustain."

He turned away and walked back to the granite table. He touched the big screen and its display changed to show multiple graphs. "Take a look at this," he said. "You notice the common trend in all of them?"

The labels on the graphs were too small to read but Noah could make out the lines connecting the data points. "They all show a steep rise in the Y-axis over the X."

"Indeed they do. Now, let me magnify this graph here. X is Time, while Y is temperature. The dates go all the way back to the eighteenth century. This point in time," he indicated a spot with his index finger, "is the beginning of the Industrial Revolution, which is when the temperature begins to increase. The Industrial Revolution brought new technological advancements to boost agricultural output and manufactured goods, urbanizing cities to what they are today. With innovation came an increase in pollution to the land, seas, and skies. You can see how the temperature rises continuously over time. Technological advancements bring many gains, but not without a cost. Climate change was pushed aside time and again by the greed of our species, deferred for the next generation to deal with it. Why worry about the future when we can enjoy the here and now? Well, the time for change came at C0+, when the G7 governments finally acted. Do you see what I'm getting at?"

"You're telling us that your motives are environmental?" Vizor said. He was breathing heavily through his bloodied nose and mouth. "The G7 released the deadliest biological weapon ever created to protect the Earth? Bullshit!"

Talbot eyed him with distaste. "Climate change threatened our basic needs," he said. "The data from extrapolations and simulations shows what would've happened if climate change had remained unchecked. Our fresh air would've been exhausted, our oceans polluted, our fresh water depleted, our animals extinct, our forests barren. Famine and pestilence would've reigned. Let me be very clear—climate change was a threat far worse than anything the world had faced before. The creation of COVID-19 was a godsend for humanity. Because of it and its mutated strains, we have defeated climate change, and our species will prosper for another thousand millennia."

"You're a maniac!" Noah shouted. "There must've been another way than an eternal pandemic!"

"None that would've worked quickly enough," Talbot said calmly.

"You robbed the world of its freedom," Noah said. "How can you live with that?"

"You're a naïve child," he spat at Noah. "What do you know of the world? You're too young to remember when governments genuinely discussed the colonization of our species on distant planets, as if the Earth were too late to save. Everything the G7 did was for the prosperity of humankind on this planet.

"The Paris Agreement of C4— reversed our course for catastrophe. The development of a lethal COVID-19 virus eliminated airline companies, reduced daily vehicle commutes, strangled polluting local businesses, which in turn caused people to isolate within their own homes, therefore reducing our global carbon footprint dramatically. The international treaty on climate change didn't simply meet its goal of limiting global warming below two degrees compared to pre-industrial levels—it *surpassed* them. The G7 achieved a climate neutral world well before mid-century!"

"But what did any of this have to do with China?" Eamon said. "Why cripple them instead of other big polluting countries like Brazil or India?"

"They were not only one of the leading polluters of the twenty-first century but also a risk to the G7 nations. China was never going to cooperate with us, not with their communist ways; their republic was a welcome sacrifice to The Great Reset."

"That doesn't make it right," Noah said. "The planet may be saved, but the damage you've caused is immeasurable. While you've been living in your high castles, so many have suffered."

Talbot rolled his eyes. "Spare me the sad songs. No one sees the bright side of things anymore. Natural disasters are at an all-time low, ocean levels have normalized, the ice caps are growing, previously endangered species are thriving, and our lands have never prospered more. The caging of man was the best thing that ever happened to this planet."

Talbot checked the time on his watch. "But alas, I've said too much. The time for talk is over." He regarded the group. "Now you know the truth. And now you must die."

Eamon leaned as far toward Goodwill as he could. "Did you catch all that?" he whispered.

Noah looked from his father to Goodwill, whose usual dark, translucent eyes were still translucent, but now pearly. Noah's mind flashed back to the blonde news anchor he'd watched so many times on TV, with her prominent cheekbones and pearly, translucent eyes.

Talbot frowned. "What's this all about?" he demanded.

"Mister Prime Minister, sir," Goodwill said. "I'm sure you've heard some of my broadcasts. I'm Goddfrey Williams, aka Goodwill, from the early C10+s. I was a radio personality for years before crossing over into television. I became a media reporter and the people loved my first-person point of view."

Understanding spread across Talbot's face. "No!" he roared and his voice echoed around the dark chamber. "This can't be!"

"I gained a lot of subscribers after my surgery," Goodwill went on. "It's a risky procedure, having microchips surgically implanted into your optic nerves, but I just had to do it for my dedicated fans. Of course, I've been inactive for years, but what better time to reconnect with my subscribers than now?"

"Good luck explaining this to your associates," Eamon said.

Goodwill fixed Talbot with his pearly eyes. "Everything you've just confessed has been transmitted live, already viewed by millions around the world. And it's recorded too, for posterity." He smiled his million dollar smile.

Talbot jerked forward, hands raised as if he might choke each and every one of them to death. The drones spun lazily toward him, guns aimed at his chest and head. He stared up at them, wide-eyed, and slowly sank to his knees, hands behind his head. The fire in his steel-grey eyes were extinguished.

Noah peered at his dad, and a smile crept onto his face. "We did it," he said. "We actually did it."

Chapter Forty-Two

Noah sat at the white kitchen counter at home, his tablet in front of him. It was four months after the events in the House of Commons. And his nineteenth birthday.

It couldn't have been more different to his eighteenth.

He idly scrolled through the news stories on his screen and stopped when a headline suddenly caught his eye:

Retired General Handed Lifetime Sentence for War Crimes

Noah turned off the tablet and tossed it aside. He put his face in his hands. There was so much to celebrate now that the world knew the truth about COVID, but Noah struggled to reconcile the whole series of events in his mind. FLIGHT's operations had led to the demise not only of OWN Industries, but of the privileged elite around the world, and even the G7 tyrants themselves. Authoritarian governments had been replaced by temporary councils; doctors and scientists were asked to pave the way in liberating the world from COVID-37. Viktor Ivanov's isolation of the spike protein had led to the development of a cure and the pharmaceutical company Mesiha&Co were producing stockpiles of the vaccine around the clock, while their stocks launched to the moon. Initial vaccine trials showed great promise, with minimal side effects and efficacy rates around 98%.

Noah had received his one-dose vaccine three days earlier and his left shoulder was still sore from the needle poke. He'd never even imagined disposing of his HAZMAT suit, but now he breathed the open air without protection or concern. The vaccine roll-out had been rapid and while there were skeptics who questioned the safety of the vaccine despite the scientific evidence—perhaps understandably distrustful of their new scientific leaders after being manipulated for so long by those in power— the majority welcomed the new vaccine. They lined up outside vaccination clinics in droves, awaiting their turn to gain immunity and freedom, and to dispose of their Distance Bands.

But despite all this optimism, Noah couldn't shake the sadness looming over him. He wanted to be happy—he practiced gratitude and mindfulness exercises daily, to remind himself of his good fortune—but he hadn't quite achieved the happy ending he'd wanted.

He stood up and grabbed his jacket and boots before moving through the dormant Disinfectant Chamber. He opened the front door and stepped out onto the porch. It was a rare warm November day, with a soft wind gently moving the air. He went down the driveway and trudged along the snowy sidewalk, passing families and couples bundled up in their winter gear. Across the street, a car pulled into a driveway and Noah watched as a young woman ran out of the house to greet an elderly woman getting out the car. They embraced for some time, heedless of any social distancing, unfettered by HAZMAT suits.

The new world, Noah thought.

Exactly one year ago, his grandparents had passed away. His remaining grandfather, a man he hadn't even known of previously, had been sentenced to life in prison for his role in The Great Reset. Noah had attended General Vizor's court appearance only yesterday, when the verdict was hammered down. Vizor hadn't been surprised by the decision, nor had he been disappointed by it. In fact, Noah had sensed a certain serenity wash over the General as he was escorted from the courtroom in handcuffs. Before the doors had closed behind him, Vizor had shot Noah a curt nod.

Noah arrived at the local grocery store, a fifteen-minute walk from his home. He grabbed the door handle and pushed it open, though it had taken some time getting used to touching public surfaces with his bare hands. He still carried a little bottle of hand sanitizer in his pocket, to apply after touching things. He strolled down an aisle, looking for snacks before his afternoon classes began. He'd enrolled himself back on his degree in Physiology and Pharmacology, with all classes still being offered virtually. There'd been talk of reopening classrooms next semester, once enough students were immunized to COVID-37, but for now, the Hover helmet was there to stay.

Every time Noah donned his Hover helmet, he was overwhelmed with memories of the Simulation Chamber, and the grief of losing Nikita and Cecilia. With social distancing measures lifted, Noah had the opportunity to go on dates with girls for the first time in his life, but Cecilia was so prominent in his mind there was no room for anyone else. Yes, she betrayed FLIGHT, but his head couldn't reason with his heart. She was etched into his soul forever.

Noah heard a cough from the next aisle over and he froze, his pulse quickening. The other shoppers froze too. Noah peered around the end of the aisle and saw a middle-aged man with beady eyes in a button-up shirt and jeans. His cheeks were flushed.

"Sorry, that's just my asthma acting up," the man said and laughed awkwardly. He waved a card at the staring shoppers. "Don't worry, I got my immunization status right here."

Old habits die hard, Noah thought. It was going to take a while for people to think of a cough as merely a cough.

He gathered his snacks and walked over to the till. The cashier was an older Hispanic gentleman with weary eyes, as if he had lost so much over the years. He wore a purple bandana over his mouth and nose.

"Maria, I need you to grab more bags when you have a minute, *por favor*," he said to the woman behind him. She wore a blossom red bandana over her lower face.

"You got it, *mi amor*," she said in a voice as smooth as honey. She turned around, flipped her dark brown hair, and kissed her husband through their bandanas.

Noah stared at the man's name tag, then his wife's.

Noah spoke, hesitantly. "Mr. and Mrs. Flores?"

Chapter Forty-Three

Eamon's car was on the driveway when Noah got home. He went inside and dumped his snacks on the kitchen counter.

"You're home early today," Noah said.

His father was on the couch in the living room, watching TV. "I locked up the clinic doors already. Turns out I didn't have that many belongings in my office."

Noah opened a bag of chips and stood next to the couch, watching the screen. "Looks like Goodwill is doing well for himself," he said and crunched on a chip.

"He's in his element," Eamon said. "*The False Truth* has topped the ratings for the past four months."

"I'm glad everything worked out for at least one of us."

Eamon sighed then stood up from the couch and clutched Noah's shoulder. "Listen, son. I know this is really difficult for you, and I'm sorry things had to end this way."

"Why can't they be more understanding? If it wasn't for you, there wouldn't be a vaccine. The world would still be controlled by OWN and the G7. *You* got us out of that mess. Can't they just wash away the charges over Villa Salud?"

"I'm afraid not. When I signed up for FLIGHT, I knew there were risks for both of us. I did everything for the greater good, nothing more."

"First General Vizor, now you," Noah said. "I want to be there for your trial tomorrow, but a part of me doesn't want to see it play out. I don't know what I'll do without you, Dad."

"You have to be strong, son. When things change, we adjust and keep moving forward. That's how humans have always survived." He patted Noah's arm. "I've deposited enough money into your savings account over the years for you to live comfortably enough. Whatever you decide to do, with school or otherwise, do it proudly and courageously. You'll be able to visit me, and I'll write often."

Noah looked miserably into the depths of his bag of chips.

"This is what your grandparents died for, Noah. A world free from COVID-37, a world you can explore, find love, pursue your passions, continue changing things for the better."

Eamon was right; things hadn't turned out the way he'd hoped, but the risks they'd taken had been for the greater good, for the betterment of generations to come. But his father would still spend the rest of his life in jail.

"Come with me," Eamon said. "Let tomorrow's worries be tomorrow's worries. I've got you a little something." He went into the kitchen and Noah followed him. "Happy nineteenth birthday, son."

He took a black velvet box from his pocket and placed it on the countertop. Noah opened it, but he knew what it contained. On a soft, white satin cushion lay a silver necklace of The Cross.

"My gift from last year," Noah said. "I thought it was lost."

"Well, we had other things on our minds," Eamon said and grinned. "I grabbed it from your pocket that first night at FLIGHT, when you were recovering in the patient observation unit. I held onto it, for safe keeping."

Noah rolled the jewelry around his fingers. "What's this about anyway? You've never been a religious man."

"True. But your grandparents were devout Catholics. You remember the stories they used to tell you." He touched the necklace in Noah's hand, briefly and lightly. "There's one more thing to go along with it." He opened the cupboard under the counter and removed another box, about eight inches square, made of glossy wood with The Cross outlined on the lid. Each arm of The Cross had a tiny hole engraved into it with speakers around the sides of the box.

"Dad, what in the world is this thing?"

Eamon turned the box carefully to face Noah. "A company called Soul Inc. has developed a technology called the Spirit-Keeper." He put his index finger on the box. "Your grandparents knew how much you enjoyed visiting them every year and they also knew they weren't going to be around forever. So, they got in touch with Soul Inc. and signed up to digitize a part of themselves inside this Spirit-Keeper."

Noah picked up the box and raised it to his eyes. He stared at it long enough for his father to be able to read his thoughts. "Your mother, Olivia . . . she isn't in there. The company has only been around for the last four years. After her time."

Noah nodded. "So, this thing contains Grandpa John and Grandma Noelle?"

"In a sense. They consented for their complete digital history to be uploaded into this device. Think of it like Siri but personalized to be your grandparents. It does require additional pieces, though." Eamon reached into his pant's pocket and pulled out two more crosses, just like Noah's. "I grabbed these back at Villa Salud as we were leaving." He inserted the foot of each cross into two of the holes on the Spirit-Keeper's lid. The box emanated a bluish-yellow aura.

"Whoa," Noah said and held the device at arm's length.

"You'll be able to communicate with them anytime you like," Eamon said, indicating The Cross still looped around Noah's fingers. "Give it a try."

Noah put the box down and removed the necklace over his head. He held The Cross tightly and inserted its foot into the bottom hole of the Spirit-Keeper.

Suddenly, the speakers hummed to life. From the depths of the box, two voices awoke.

"I knew we'd meet again, my dear boy," Grandpa John said.

"Happy birthday, sweetie," Grandma Noelle said.

"Grandma? Grandpa? Is it really you?" He leaned closer to the Spirit-Keeper.

"As real as we can be," they answered together.

Grandpa John asked, "Has it really been a whole year since we last spoke?"

"It really has," Noah said. "And a lot has changed, now that we're in the year 2070."

Manufactured by Amazon.ca
Bolton, ON